即選即用
商用英語會話

English at Work : Everyday Business
Conversation Samples

李普生 著

五南圖書出版公司 印行

序言
Preface

　　每個人學習語言固然有自己不同的動機和適應上的問題，但若不能不斷提升精進任何已凝聚的成效和結果，運氣好的原地踏步，運氣不好的回到原點！

　　學習英語文的唯一訣竅在於不斷地努力，雖是老生常談，但它的意義卻不減。如何找到誘因（或驅策的力量），如何發掘興趣，如何在有時嫌單調的過程中找到樂趣，如何與現今環境結合，如何在工作中實際使用？因衝擊而找到啟發，從靜滯不前到勇敢嘗試，只要不斷地學和反覆地說，掌握語言並使其成為自己競爭時的利器絕非不可能！

　　本書的主人翁是一名經由面談而進入本地一家外商公司的專業人，透過不同的情境，如：走馬上任、與上司同事和下屬相處、問題處理、交際應酬、外調差遣等，經由與不同角色人物之間的運作，他學會如何利用英語來說明、提問、反駁、妥協。如果經由本書主人翁的境遇

和遭遇能對所有讀者的衝擊和刺激提供反思和進一步學習的誘因，那本書編撰的目的也就達到了！

　　本書共有十六個單元，除了第一單元面試（因面試中出現的問題和情境，與其他主題相比變化性並不大）之外，每單元中都有三段範文，每段範文後設計有「譯文」、「詞彙片語」、「小提醒」、「練習」、「換種說法」和「練習解答」等小主題，各個小主題的編排設計說明如下：

> 範文：三段連續式的對話，將與主題相關情境中會有的對話內容分
　　　　別列出。

> 譯文：範文對話的中文對照，可以協助讀者掌握內容。

> 詞彙片語：依照出現順序相關的用詞、片語都有簡易的說明。

> 小提醒：除了將與範文中相關或重要的文法觀念，以提綱挈領的方
　　　　　式做複習之外，文化資訊和常識也是編寫重點。

> 練習：對範文中所提到的內容，利用問答方式，確認讀者的理解程

度，也同時做書寫的練習。

> 換種說法：將同樣主題以不同的方式表達或將可能產生的後續發
　　　　　展，利用對話方式提供讀者參考。

> 練習解答：將正確的回答方法列出，供讀者自行更正。

　　透過這些不同的學習活動，編者不僅希望讀者能充分了解整個相
關主題的內涵，也可確實掌握不同的表達和基本常識。

李普生

目錄
contents

目錄
contents

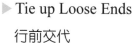

目錄
contents

目錄
contents

Job Interview

面試 (1)

Sample Conversation 範文

(Steve Lee is getting ready for a job interview tomorrow. He is talking to his friend Jack Wang.)

 Jack I have a feeling that you'll get the job.

 Steve Thanks, but it's easy for you to say; I'm not that sure about it.

 Jack Just remember to be as professional and polite as you can. Oh, one more thing, don't forget to smile!

 Steve I'll try, but sometimes I found it's hard to be myself when I am in stressful or even dire situations!

 Jack How about your résumé? Did you update it before you sent it out?

 Steve Yes...ah! I forgot to include my mailing address.

 Jack You'd better double- and triple-check everything. You also want to make sure that there are no typos that will embarrass you. Otherwise, you might shoot yourself in the foot!

 Steve That I will not, I assure you.

 Steve I wonder what I should wear: a three-piece suit, maybe?

 Jack Sounds good to me. What about your reference letters?

 Steve I got them right here in the portfolio with me. Those are from the people who can vouch for my professional experience, integrity and good

work ethic.

 Jack So, I guess you are all set for the big day!

Translation 譯文

（Steve Lee 正在為明天的面試做準備，並與他的友人 Jack Wang 談話。）

Jack 我有一種感覺，你會得到這份工作。

Steve 謝了，但你說來容易，我自己倒是沒把握！

Jack 只要記住要儘可能專業和有禮貌。對了，還有一件事，別忘了微笑。

Steve 我會努力，但有時在壓力大或可怕的情形下，想要做自己很難！

Jack 你的履歷表呢？在你寄出前有沒有更新？

Steve 有…啊！我忘了附上郵寄住址。

Jack 你最好一而再，再而三檢查。你也要確定沒有會讓你尷尬的錯字，否則，你就糗大了！

Steve 這我保證不會。

Steve 我不知要穿什麼，三件式西裝，好嗎？

Jack 聽起來不錯。你的推薦信怎樣？

Steve 我放在我資料中，那是由能擔保我的專業經驗、個人操守和工作道德的人寫的。

Jack 我想你已準備妥當了。

Words & Phrases 詞彙片語

💬 get ready for 準備妥當

- as professional and polite as you can 儘可能既專業又有禮貌
- stressful 緊張的；壓力大的
- dire 可怕的
- situation 情形；情況
- résumé 履歷（英式英文或用 C/V: Curriculum Vitae）
- mailing address 通信住址
  E-mail address 電子信箱
  permanent address 戶籍地
- double- and triple-check 檢查兩次；檢查三次；反覆檢查
- make sure 確定
- typo (=typography) 打字錯誤
- embarrass 使 … 困窘；難為情
- shoot oneself in the foot 粗心大意；笨手笨腳
- three-piece 三件式（西裝上衣、西褲和小背心）西裝
  two-piece 成套的西裝
- reference letter 推薦信
- portfolio 文件夾；公事包；投資組合
- vouch for 擔保
- professional 專業的
- integrity 誠實；正直
- ethic 道德
- all set 準備妥當

◀ A reminder 小提醒

在使用英文時常聽到有人用「as possible as」這個表達，如：

> I would like to be a conscientious（誠實）worker as possible as I can.
> 我想要儘可能地成為一名誠實的工作者。

實際上，這種說法應該是受到中文表達影響而有的中式英文！正確的用法應遵循下列的句型：

as + adj./adv. + as possible

如：

> I want to be by your side as soon as possible.
> 我要儘快地在你身邊。
> I will hand in my report as thorough as possible.
> 我將會繳交最詳盡的報告。

母語干擾（language interference）層出不窮，一不小心就會出現類似的用法，所以口語或文字表達時都要謹慎！

Job Interview

面試 (2)

 Sample Conversation 範文

(Steve Lee has arrived at the ABC Company for his job interview. As he comes in the door, the receptionist greets him.)

 Receptionist Good morning, and welcome to ABC Company. How can I help you?

 Steve And a good morning to you, too. My name is Steve Lee. I have an appointment with Mrs. Jean Patrick, the personnel manager.

 Receptionist Are you here for the interview?

 Steve Yes, I am.

 Receptionist Please take a seat and fill out this application form.

Steve Sure. Thanks.

(A woman is passing through.)

 Steve Hello, Mrs. Patrick. My name is Steve Lee. I am here for the interview. Though I don't have many sales experiences, I'm a quick learner and I believe I'm the man for the job; I can sell anything!

 Woman That's great, but I'm Ms. Smith, head of the Global Marketing, not our personnel manager.

 Steve: Oh, I'm so sorry. I was too anxious about my interview for a sales position here at your company.

 Woman: That's perfectly OK. You certainly seem confident enough to tackle everything.

Translation 譯文

（Steve Lee 到達 ABC 公司參加面試，接待員在他進門時和他打招呼。）

 Receptionist: 早安，歡迎到 ABC 公司。我能為您效勞嗎？

 Steve: 妳也早。我是 Steve Lee，我和人事經理 Jean Patrick 女士有約。

Receptionist: 您是來面試的嗎？

 Steve: 是的，我是。

Receptionist: 請坐並請填好這份表格。

Steve: 沒問題，謝謝！

（一名女子通過。）

 Steve: 您好，Patrick 女士。我的名字是 Steve Lee，我來這面試，雖然我沒有很多銷售經驗，但我學得很快而且我有自信我是這工作的最佳人選，我什麼東西都能賣！

 Woman: 那很棒，但我是 Smith 小姐，負責全球行銷部門，不是人事經理。

 Steve: 噢，我很抱歉。我等不及參加貴公司業務工作的面試了。

 Woman: 別放在心上，你看起來的確在處理所有事物上很有自信。

Words & Phrases 詞彙片語

- receptionist 接待員

- greet 迎接；招呼

- appointment 會面的約定

- personnel 人事

  （許多公司會將人事部門的稱謂用「人力資源」Human Resources 來代替）

- take a seat 就座

- fill out（完全）填妥

  （有別於 fill in 填入：Fill out the form and make sure you fill in all the blanks.）

- pass through 通過

- global 全球的

- anxious 渴望的；焦慮的；迫不急待的

- position 職務

  （求職時的職缺可用 opening: Is there any job openings in your company?）

- tackle 處理；應付

A reminder 小提醒

不論是口語表達或書寫文字，英文中有一個萬靈丹──片語。在範文中，我們已經看到了「pass through」這個片語，實際上，與 pass 相關的片語還有很多，像：

1. pass away: 去世

   The old ex-CEO passed away at the age of 90.

   前任執行長 90 歲時過世。

   (CEO: Chief Executive Officer)

2. pass down: 傳遞

   Customs and traditions are passed down from generation to generation.

   習俗和傳統代代相傳。

3. pass over: 略過

   Never pass over a word that you do not understand.

   切勿放過你不了解的字。

4. pass up: 放棄

   The job offering is too good a chance to pass up.

   這工作放棄太可惜了。

5. make a pass: 對 … 獻殷勤

   Jack always makes a pass to pretty girls.

   Jack 總是對漂亮小姐獻殷勤。

若有時間，你可以上網或經由字典查到許多有趣且實用的片語！

Job Interview

面試 (3)

Sample Conversation 範文

(Steve Lee is going through the interview of his lifetime!)

Jean Hello, I'm Jean Patrick, personnel manager. It's very nice to meet you this morning. Please follow me back to my office. Could I offer you a coffee or a soft drink?

Steve Thank you, Mrs. Patrick. It's very nice to be here. I appreciate the opportunity to speak with you this morning. Thank you for the offer of coffee, but I'm just fine right now.

Jean Have a seat; I'd like to ask you a few questions this morning if I may. Tell me a little about yourself. What do you like to do in and out of school? How would you describe the way you deal with people?

Steve Thank you for the opportunity to meet you today. I would describe myself as a typical youngster. I enjoy school, extracurricular activities, and I had worked a few hours a week after school. Dealing with people is one of my strongest points, as I seldom find someone I cannot work with. I have many friends at school and get along with all kinds of people while working part-time.

Jean What makes you interested in sales as a place to start your career? Have you ever had any sales experience?

Steve ▷ I have sales experience in several areas, from selling tickets for the school clubs to my experience in working in a convenience store. I'm interested in a sales career because I enjoy working with people, and I'm looking for a position which offers both personal and professional growth.

Translation 譯文

（Steve Lee 將要經歷他一生中最重要的面試！）

Jean ▷ 你好，我是人事經理 Jean Patrick，很高興今早見到你。請隨我到我的辦公室，要不要喝杯咖啡或其他飲料？

Steve ▷ 謝謝您，Patrick 女士。很高興來這裡，謝謝您給我今早和您見面的機會。謝謝您的咖啡的提議，但現在不用。

Jean ▷ 請坐。如果可以，我今早想請問你幾個問題，請簡單地自我介紹。你在校內校外喜歡做些什麼？描述一下你怎麼待人處世的？

Steve ▷ 謝謝您今天和我見面。我會用「典型年輕人」來形容自己，我喜歡學校和課外活動，而且我每星期也在放學後工作幾小時，因為我幾乎沒遇過我無法相處的人，所以和人相處是我的強項。我在學校有很多朋友而且打工時我和各種人都處得很好。

Jean ▷ 是什麼原因讓你選擇以業務工作開始你的職業生涯？你有任何銷售經驗嗎？

Steve ▷ 我在幾個領域有過銷售經驗，從我為學校社團賣票到在超商工作。我對業務工作感興趣是因為我喜歡和其他人一起工作，而且我也在尋找能讓我在個人和專業上都能成長的工作。

Words & Phrases 詞彙片語

- lifetime 一生
- offer 提供；給予
- soft drink 汽水；不含酒精的飲料
- right now 現在
- would like to 想要

  (= feel like to; would like to + V(原形), feel like to + V-ing)

- describe 描述
- deal with 處理；操作

  (= handle)

- opportunity 機會
- typical 典型的

  (= standard, everyday)

- extracurricular activities 課外活動
- after school 課後；課餘
- get along with 和 … 處得來
- part-time 兼差；兼職
- career 職涯
- area 領域；區域；地區
- club 社團
- convenience store 便利商店
- professional 專業的
- growth 成長

◀ A reminder 小提醒

不論是職場上的老將（seasoned worker）或是剛上陣的新手（rookie/novice），面談是少不了的步驟。在英語面試中，下列題目出現的頻率較高：

- Tell me something about yourself.
- Tell me something about your greatest achievement so far.
- Why do you want to leave your previous job?
- Do you take your work home often?
- How do you deal with stress in your work life?
- Why do you want to join our organization?
- What goals have you set for the next three years?
- How do you prepare yourself to make path（佈局）to reach goals?
- What is your definition about the ideal job?
- What are the major challenges that you have encountered so far in your career?

上述問題未必一定會在面談中出現，但知己知彼，多一分準備就會多一分收穫，更何況這份收穫是找到個好工作呢！

Job Interview

面試 (4)

Sample Conversation 範文

(There are more to come in the interview.)

Jean > It sounds like you've had interesting experiences; I appreciate your honesty. Would you describe yourself as a punctual person? How would you rate your English and computer skills compared to others in your class?

Steve > I have always been an early riser and enjoyed getting to school on time. I don't think I've ever been late for school. English was my favorite subject and my grades proved that I am a good student. As for computer skills, I have taken several computer courses and feel my skills are among the best in my class.

Jean > Unfortunately, many young people do not develop a strong commitment to their work, how will you be different? Why should I hire you for this position?

Steve > Sticking with a job to its completion is a value I truly believe in. I've learned through my school studies that the only way to succeed is to do the best job from the beginning to end. You should hire me for this job because I am the type of person you need to continue your success. I'm a hard worker who learn quickly, and I have the personal

motivation to get the job done right.

 I enjoyed our conversation today. Thank you for your answers. We have several days of interviews scheduled for the position, so I will be in touch with you over the course of the next several weeks. Good-bye.

 I have enjoyed the opportunity to learn more about your company. I look forward to hearing from you soon. Again, thank you for taking the time to see me today.

Translation 譯文

（面試還沒結束呢！）

 聽起來你有些相當有趣的經驗。謝謝你的坦白，你覺得自己是個準時的人嗎？和班上其他人相比，你會如何評量自己的英文和電腦能力呢？

 我一向是個早起而且喜歡準時到校的人。我不認為我曾經遲到過，英文是我喜歡的科目而我的成績能證明我是個好學生，至於電腦能力，我選過幾堂電腦課也覺得我是班上技巧最好的人之一。

 很遺憾，現今許多年輕人對工作不投入，你和他們不同的地方在哪裡？我為何該聘你做這工作呢？

 做事有始有終是我向來秉持的信念。我從學校學到成功的唯一之道就是從頭到尾把事情做好，您該僱用我，因為我是貴公司持續成功會需要的那種人，我是個努力工作且學得快的人，而且我有把事情做好的個人動機。

 我很喜歡我們今天的談話，謝謝你的回答。我們為了這職務安排了幾天的面試，所以我會在未來幾星期內再和你聯絡。

Steve 我也很高興能有多了解貴公司的機會，我期待能很快得到您的回音，再次謝謝您今天撥冗見我。

Words & Phrases 詞彙片語

- more to come 好戲要上演
- appreciate 感謝；欣賞
- honesty 誠實
- describe 描述；形容
- punctual 準時的
- rate 認為；被評價為
- late for 遲到
- favorite 最喜歡的 (n.: 喜歡的事物)
- subject 科目；主題
- grades 成績；分數
- unfortunately 不幸地；遺憾地
- commitment 承諾；承擔義務；獻身
- hire 聘僱
- stick with 堅持
- completion 完成；結束
- value 價值
- believe in 信仰，信任；認為有價值的
- personal 個人的
- motivation 動機；誘因
- get the job done 把事情做好
- schedule 安排

● be in touch with 接觸;聯絡

● over the course of 在 … 的時間裡

● look forward to 盼望;期待

● take the time 花時間

A reminder 小提醒

就像書寫英文時一樣,說英語時也會因人、事、物的不同而有正式和非正式用法之分:

1. 非正式用法

   A: Jean, I lost my calculator. Mind if I use yours?

   B: No, not at all. You can have it.

   A: OK if I have it until this evening?

   B: Oh, sure.

2. 正式用法

   A: Good morning, sir.

   B: Good morning. Have you got the confirmation (確認) from the speaker for the ceremony (典禮)?

   A: Yes, sir. Professor Mathew from St. Joseph's College has given his consent (同意). He'll reach here by 9 am tomorrow. Would it be possible to send the car to pick him up?

   B: I'm afraid it is impossible. You'd better hire a taxi. We'll pay the fare (車資).

經由上述的例證,我們可以知道「和什麼人說什麼話」這句俗語的箇中真諦!

First Day on the Job

第一天上班 (1)

🔘 Sample Conversation 範文

(Steve Lee, now a veteran manager, is going to meet his new boss, Paul Jones.)

Paul Welcome aboard, Steve.

Steve Thank you. I'm delighted to be working here. Mr. Jones.

Paul You were the perfect man for the job and we're so happy to have you with us. By the way, call me Paul, will you?

Steve I feel a bit of awkward calling you by your first name. It sounds, how should I put it, disrespectful.

Paul Don't worry. Everybody in the company all the way up to and down the line is called by their first name, OK?

Steve I'll try.

Paul Good. Oh, but in the presence of outsiders in formal business situations, it may be a good idea to address your higher-ups as Mr., Ms., or whatever is appropriate, understand?

Steve Yes, sir.

Paul And don't "sir" me either. You seem nervous.

Steve Well, I do have butterflies.

Paul Everybody's like that on their first day. You'll get over it soon. Now I'll show you your office.

Steve ⟩ It's such a nice office.

Paul ⟩ This is your secretary, Nancy Chen. She's been with the company for years. And she's a perfect bilingual.

(Translation 譯文

（經驗豐富的經理 Steve Lee 將要見他的新老闆 Paul Jones。）

Paul ⟩ Steve，歡迎加入我們的行列。

Steve ⟩ 謝謝，Jones 先生，我很高興能到這工作。

Paul ⟩ 你是這工作最適當的人選，我們很高興能有你加入我們。對了，叫我 Paul，好嗎？

Steve ⟩ 我覺得直呼你名字有些怪，該怎麼說呢，聽起來有些不敬。

Paul ⟩ 別擔心！公司每個人從上到下都是直呼其名，好嗎？

Steve ⟩ 我試試看。

Paul ⟩ 好。對了，但在正式場合和外人面前，用先生女士或其他適當頭銜來稱呼你的上司會較恰當。

Steve ⟩ 遵命。

Paul ⟩ 還有，別跟我來遵命這套，你看起來很緊張。

Steve ⟩ 我心中的確七上八下。

Paul ⟩ 每個人第一天報到時都是如此，你很快就會習慣的。現在，我帶你去你的辦公室。

Steve ⟩ 這辦公室很棒。

Paul ⟩ 這是你的祕書 Nancy Chen，她待在公司很多年了，而且她中英兩種語言都非常流利。

Words & Phrases 詞彙片語

- veteran 經驗豐富的

- in store for 即將發生；等待

- welcome aboard 歡迎加入

- be delighted to 很高興…

- by the way 順便一提；對了

- will you? 好嗎？

- awkward 尷尬的；難處理的

- first name: (= given name, forename) 名字

  姓：last name, surname, family name

- disrespectful 不敬的

- all the way up 一路向上

- down the line 往下；完全地

- in the presence of 在…面前

- outsiders 外人；局外人

- situation 形勢；局面

- a good idea to 好主意

- address 稱呼

- higher-up 上級；大人物

- appropriate 適當的；合宜的

- nervous 緊張的

- butterfly 做重要事情前的忐忑不安

  have butterflies in one's stomach 因緊張而胃部翻騰

- get over 克服；恢復常態
- perfect 完美的；精通的
- bilingual 能說兩種語言的人

◀ A reminder 小提醒

「Welcome aboard」原本用在服務人員對搭船、登機或上車的客人的問候語，現在也成為公司裡歡迎新進人員到職的歡迎詞。在英文中有許多從不同領域「借」來的表達，像：

> break a leg 若先祝福旅者跌斷腿，在旅程中就不會有壞事了；祝好運
> on the money（來自美式足球）沒有浪費賭注；完全正確的
> under par（來自高爾夫球）在標準桿下；失常演出
> tie-breaker（來自網球）平手勝局；打破僵局的關鍵
> throw a curve ball（來自棒球）投了個曲球；意外之舉

俗語說：「人生如戲」，但在英文的使用上，尤其是美式英文，「人生如球戲」倒顯得更恰當！文化資訊的知識和掌握與英文學習之間是息息相關的。這裡再次證明光是看懂字絕不代表了解意思！

✎ Exercise 練習

利用括弧中所提供的字來改寫句子：

① You were the perfect man for the job.

(more qualified, to get, than)

❷ I feel awkward calling you by your first name.

(embarrassed, as Paul, addressing)

❸ You'll get over it soon.

(before long, return to normal)

☼ Say It Differently 換種說法

Paul Good to have you aboard.

Steve Thank you very much. I'm happy to be here.

Paul Excited?

Steve Very.

Paul Relax/Don't be.

Paul Even though everybody's quite friendly here, it's not good to be too familiar with your superiors. Does that make sense to you?

Steve Yes, it does. Thank for your advice.

Paul Not at all. I'll take you to your office.

Translation 譯文

Paul 很高興你能加入公司。

Steve 非常謝謝你，我很高興能在這裡。

Paul 很興奮嗎？

Steve 非常興奮。

Paul 放輕鬆／別。

Paul 雖然這裡所有人都很友善，但和上司太熟不是件好事，你懂嗎？

 Steve > 是的，的確如此。謝謝你的建議。

 Paul > 別客氣，現在我帶你去你的辦公室。

✱ before long 不久；很快地

✱ relax 放輕鬆

✱ friendly 友善的

✱ be too familiar with 交往過密；太熟

✱ make sense 有道理

Answer Key 練習解答

❶ You were more qualified than anyone else to get the job.

❷ I feel embarrassed addressing you as Paul.

❸ You'll return to normal before long.

First Day on the Job

第一天上班 (2)

◐ Sample Conversation 範文

(Paul Jones is showing Steve Lee around.)

Nancy Hello, how do you do. Mr. Lee?

Steve How do you do.

Paul Nancy, tell Steve how to fill out the expense sheets after I've taken him around.

Nancy Certainly. Let me know if you have questions.

Paul Nancy's been here for 10 years. She knows the company inside and out. Now I'll show you your way around and let you get your bearings.

Steve My bearings?

Paul Oh, that's just a colloquial expression. It means knowing which way is which.

Steve Oh, I see.

Paul Here. This is your program for the week.

Steve My program?

Paul Yes, you'll spend most of this week talking to different line managers, learning about their functions in the organization.

Steve Great!

Paul〉 Before I forget, let's have lunch together today. I can tell you about good eating places in the neighborhood. Now I'll give you a quick tour of the offices. This is our company cafeteria. I'll show you the ropes... .

Translation 譯文

（Paul Jones 帶 Steve Lee 四處看看。）

Nancy〉 你好，Lee 先生？

Steve〉 妳好。

Paul〉 Nancy，我帶 Steve 四處看看後，教他如何填寫費用表。

Nancy〉 好的，如果你有問題就告訴我。

Paul〉 Nancy 已在公司十年，她對公司裡裡外外都很了解。現在，我帶你四處看看讓你熟悉環境。

Steve〉 熟悉環境？

Paul〉 噢，只不過是句口頭禪，讓你知道哪是哪。

Steve〉 知道了。

Paul〉 這裡是你這星期的行程。

Steve〉 我的行程？

Paul〉 是的，你這星期大部分時間都會花在和不同基層經理晤談，了解他們在公司裡負責的工作。

Steve〉 好極了！

Paul〉 先說免得我忘記，我們今天一起吃午餐。我可以告訴你這附近哪裡有好吃的。現在我很快地帶你去看看其他辦公室，這是公司的自助餐廳，

我會告訴你一些公司內部的事 …。

Words & Phrases 詞彙片語

- show...around 參觀一下
- expense sheets 費用表
- inside and out 裡裡外外
- one's bearings 方向；熟悉環境
- colloquial 口語的
- expression 表達；說詞
- program 程序表；節目單
- line managers 部門經理；基層負責人
- function 職務；功能；作用
- neighborhood 附近
- show one the ropes 教以方法；告知內情

A reminder 小提醒

「let's」是「let us」的縮寫，否定的寫法是「let us not」「let's not.」在美式口語表達中也會使用「don't let's」或「let's don't.」。以 let's 開頭的句子，若改成附加問句，要寫成 shall we？但 let 開頭的句子則要寫成 will you？
如：

Let us not have lunch together.
Don't let's have lunch together.

Unit 2

Let's not have lunch together.

Let's have lunch together, shall we?

Let him have lunch with us, will you?

Exercise 練習

利用括弧中所提供的字來改寫句子：

❶ Tell Steve how to fill out the expense sheets.

(show, do his)

❷ Nancy knows the company inside and out.

(Nancy doesn't know, nothing)

❸ I can tell you about good eating places in the neighborhood.

(give you some tips, fine restaurants, near here)

✱ tips 提示

☀ Say It Differently 換種說法

 Paul 〉 Meet your secretary, Mrs. Nancy Chen.

 Steve 〉 Hi, I'm happy to meet you.

 Nancy 〉 Same here.

 Paul 〉 She's been here for a long time and knows everything about the company.

 Nancy 〉 Well not quite everything but I can tell you the shortest route from the

MRT station to the office.

Steve ⟩ Super, I'll see you later.

Paul ⟩ Now let us get your bearings around here.

Steve ⟩ Beg your pardon. I'm not familiar with that phrase.

Paul ⟩ To get your bearings simply means to find out where you are.

Translation 譯文

Paul ⟩ 這是你的祕書 Nancy Chen。

Steve ⟩ 嗨，很高興見到妳。

Nancy ⟩ 彼此彼此。

Paul ⟩ 她在這裡很久了，而且知道公司裡所有事。

Nancy ⟩ 不是所有事，但我可以告訴你從捷運站到公司最短的捷徑。

Steve ⟩ 棒透了，待會見。

Paul ⟩ 現在讓我們來熟悉環境。

Steve ⟩ 對不起，我不熟悉那種說法。

Paul ⟩ 熟悉環境就是知道你在哪裡。

✳ same here　彼此彼此

✳ route　途徑；路線

（本段會話中提及捷運站到公司最近的路線純屬開玩笑；只不過是用些小資訊
來加強 Nancy 對公司大事小事都了解的事實。）

✳ see you later　待會見

✳ beg one's pardon　對不起；抱歉（打擾一下）

✳ phrase 成語；慣用語

Answer Key 練習解答

❶ Show Steve how to do his expense sheets.

❷ There's nothing Nancy doesn't know about the company.

❸ I can give you some tips about the fine restaurants near here.

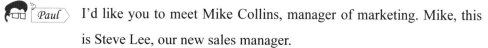

First Day on the Job

第一天上班 (3)

○ Sample Conversation 範文

(Steve is finding out more about the company for he needs to fit in right away.)

Paul   I'd like you to meet Mike Collins, manager of marketing. Mike, this is Steve Lee, our new sales manager.

Mike   Hi. It's good to have you aboard.

Steve   I'm very pleased to meet you.

Mike   You've come from International Trading Company, I believe.

Steve   That's right. I had been with them for six years.

Mike   That's an excellent company. The two organizations are now about the same size but you may find our corporate culture quite different.

Steve   In what way, if I may ask?

Mike   Well, I'd say that you'll find our management team members extremely down-to-earth and open with employees.

Paul   I agree. Also we're more aggressive than they are. And our growth record attests to that. What we have here is a more competitive work environment and more entrepreneurial spirit.

Mike   It won't take you long to get oriented to our corporate style. To say the least, you won't get bored. I'm sure you'll like it here.

Steve   Thanks. I look forward to working with you.

Translation 譯文

（Steve Lee 發現他要多對公司有些了解以便馬上融入。）

Paul 我想要你見見行銷經理 Mike Collins 先生。Mike，這是我們新的業務經理 Steve Lee。

Mike 嗨，很高興你加入公司。

Steve 我很高興見到你。

Mike 你是從國際貿易公司來的，是吧？

Steve 是的，我在那裡六年。

Mike 那是間優秀的公司，兩家公司規模相當，但你會發現我們公司間的文化大不相同。

Steve 我能問如何不同嗎？

Mike 你會發現我們的經營團隊非常務實而且對員工很開放。

Paul 我同意，同時我們也比他們更積極，我們成長的紀錄能證明：我們這裡有的是一個更具競爭性的環境和更具創業性的精神。

Mike 你很快就會熟悉我們公司的風格，至少你不會感到無聊。我很確定你會喜歡這裡。

Steve 謝謝你，我很期盼和你一起工作。

Words & Phrases 詞彙片語

- fit in 融入
- excellent 優秀的；卓越的
- size 大小；規模

Unit 2 What's in Store for Me? 不知會發生什麼。 031

- corporate culture 公司 / 組織文化
- quite 相當地；完全地
- extremely 非常地；極端地
- down-to-earth 實在的；實務的
- open 率直的；沒有隱藏的
- aggressive 積極的；有進取心的
- attest to 證明
- competitive 競爭的
- entrepreneurial spirit 企業家精神
- orient 使…熟悉
- take long to 花長時間
- say the least 至少可以這樣說
- bored 無聊的；無趣的
- style 風格；形式
- look forward to 期望；期盼

◀ A reminder 小提醒

to 可以和動詞連用成不定詞，to 也可以變成介系詞而和名詞或動名詞連用。

> V + 不定詞：agree, begin, care, choose, decide, fail, forget, guarantee, happen, love, manage, neglect, offer, plan, remember, seek, tend...
>
> V + 動名詞：avoid, consider, discuss, enjoy, finish, imagine, keep, mention, pardon, quit, risk, suggest, understand

自己進修英文時，千萬不可每回見到 to 就說成不定詞；同樣地，也不可以每回看見 to 就說它是介系詞。

✑ Exercise 練習

使用括弧中所提供的字來改寫句子：

❶ You've come from the International Trading Company, I believe.

(with, you were, I understand)

❷ Also we're more aggressive than they are.

(less aggressive, we are)

❸ It won't take you long to get oriented to our corporate style.

(get used to, you'll soon)

✱ get used to 習慣

☀ Say It Differently 換種說法

Steve ❯ I had worked at International Trading Company for six years.

Mike ❯ They're real pros in the trading business. We have something to learn from their marketing strategies too.

Steve ❯ I'm glad you feel that way.

Mike ❯ Do you know anything about the trading market?

Steve ❯ Not enough, I'm afraid. But I know the basic and I'm a quick learner.

Mike ❯ We have an "open door" policy. Any time you have a question or grievance, you can go into any executive's office.

 Paul Our management team is a bunch of top-flight people. You'll enjoy talking to them later.

Translation 譯文

 Steve 我在國際貿易公司工作了六年。

 Mike 他們在貿易上是行家，我們也可以在他們的行銷策略上學些東西。

 Steve 我很高興你有這種想法。

 Mike 你對貿易市場有多少認識？

 Steve 恐怕不夠多，但我知道基本的，而且我學得快。

 Mike 我們有一個開放政策，你有任何疑問或委屈，你可以直接進主管的辦公室講。

 Paul 我們的管理團隊是一群一流的人，你待會就會愛上和他們聊天的感覺。

* pro (=professional) 專業人士
* business 行業
* strategies 策略
* open door policy 開放政策
* grievance 冤情；委屈
* executive 主管；經理
* top-flight 第一流的

Answer Key 練習解答

❶ You were with International Trading Company I understand.

❷ Also they're less aggressive than we are.

❸ You'll soon get used to our corporate style.

Company Rules and Regulations

公司規章 (1)

Sample Conversation 範文

(Steve Lee is going to find out some facts of life in the new company.)

Ingrid I'm Ingrid Kim from General Affairs. Paul Jones has asked me to come and explain the company rules and regulations to you.

Steve I appreciate that very much, Ingrid. Please have a seat. I really need your help to learn how this company runs.

Ingrid I'd like to be of as much assistance to you as possible. If you have any questions, just ask.

Steve Here is my first question. Can I smoke?

Ingrid The whole office is smoke-free; still, you can provided you smoke in the designated areas.

Steve May I offer you a cigarette?

Ingrid No, thank you. I quit smoking years ago.

Steve I believe that each organization has its own set of unwritten rules about behavior. What may be considered "good" manners at another company could be totally unacceptable here. At my old job, they were fairly strict about requiring employees to be punctual at the beginning of the working day no matter how late they might have stayed the night before.

Translation 譯文

（Steve Lee 將要發現一些新公司的規定。）

Ingrid 我是總務處的 Ingrid Kim，Paul Jones 要我來向你解釋公司的規定。

Steve Ingrid，非常謝謝妳。請坐，我需要妳幫我了解公司是如何運作的。

Ingrid 我希望儘可能對你有幫助，有任何問題就問我。

Steve 我的第一個問題是：我能抽菸嗎？

Ingrid 整個辦公室都是禁菸，但如果在吸菸區，你可以抽菸。

Steve 我能敬妳一支菸嗎？

Ingrid 不用，謝謝你，我多年前就戒了。

Steve 我相信每個組織在應對進退上都有自己的一套潛規則，在另家公司被認為好的可能在這裡是完全不能接受。在我以前的公司，他們就在對員工不管前一天晚上待得多晚，在早上準時上班的規定上相當嚴格。

Words & Phrases 詞彙片語

- Dos & Don'ts 能做和不能做的事
- facts of life 人生中的現實面
- General Affairs 事務部；總務處 / 課
- run 經營；運作
- assistance 協助
- smoke-free 禁菸
- provided 如果；在 … 的條件下
- designated 指定的

- area 區域；地區
- offer 提供；給予
- quit 停止；中斷
- unwritten rules 潛規則
- manners 禮貌
- totally 完全地
- unacceptable 不能接受的
- fairly 相當地
- strict 嚴格的
- require 要求；命令
- punctual 準時的

A reminder 小提醒

英文中一字數義的情形相當普遍，就拿範文中的 run 來做比方：

The boy came running (跑) to me.

Vines (藤) run (蔓延) over the porch (門廊).

The politician will run (參選) for the office.

The magazine ran (報導) a story on nuclear energy (核能).

The hotel is well run (經營).

The fox ran after (追) the rabbit.

How often does the bus run (來往行駛)?

如果加上片語，run 這個字本身就會像一本字典：

run across 偶然遇到

run after 追逐

run against 撞上；違反

run away (from) 逃跑

run into 撞到

run out of 用完

run over 瀏覽

run up 高漲

學英文時最忌諱學些「大而不當」的字詞，越是簡單但卻實用的字越要把握！

 Exercise 練習

利用括弧所提供的字來改寫句子：

❶ I really need your help to learn how this company runs.

(to help me, I'd like, figure out)

❷ I'd like to be of as much assistance to you as possible.

(offer, as much help, need)

❸ If you have any questions, just ask.

(let me know, unclear to you, there's anything)

Say It Differently 換種說法

Ingrid Paul Jones asked me to give you a brief rundown about company policy.

 Steve　I'm grateful for that. I've read the policy manual but it seemed to be written in legalese.

 Ingrid　It certainly reads like that, I'm afraid. Did you have any questions?

 Steve　Yes, I have some outside business interests. Do I have to report them to the management?

 Ingrid　No, not unless you have a sizable holding in an entity that does business with the company.

Translation 譯文

 Ingrid　Paul Jones 要我給你關於公司政策的簡短說明。

 Steve　我很感謝妳，我已讀過公司政策手冊但寫得好像都是法律術語。

 Ingrid　恐怕讀起來的確如此，你有任何問題嗎？

 Steve　有，我有些公司外的業務所得，我要向管理階層報告嗎？

Ingrid　不用，除非你持有和我們公司做生意公司的鉅額股份。

* brief rundown 簡短的（逐項）說明、解釋
* policy manual 政策手冊
* legalese 法律術語
* outside business interests 公司外的業務／生意所得的收益
* management 管理階層
* sizable 相當大的
* holding 持有股份；所有權
* entity 實體（公司）

Answer Key 練習解答

❶ I'd like you to help me figure out how this company runs.

❷ I'd like to offer you as much help as you need.

❸ Let me know if there's anything unclear to you.

Company Rules and Regulations

公司規章 (2)

Sample Conversation 範文

(Steve Lee will find out that there are more benefits than he expected.)

 Steve > I suspect that's not the same here, is it?

 Ingrid > I'm glad you raised that issue, because we adopted the flex-time system here. It means that you can choose what time you are going to start and finish.

 Steve > Oh? I thought the office hours were 9:00 to 5:00.

 Ingrid > Yes, but managerial people can set their own work schedules. You don't have to start each day at the same time, but you must be here for core time, which is from 10 to 3. Also, you're expected to put in at least 37 1/2 hours a week.

 Steve > I see. Not that it matters, but do I get a yearly increase? I'm just curious.

 Ingrid > The answer is yes. Our work rules say salaries are adjusted once a year. Your immediate supervisor will review your compensation against your performance and recommend an increase. This year the average hike is three percent.

 Steve > How many days of vacation can I take in the first year?

 Ingrid > You're entitled to ten days of vacation for the balance of this year.

In addition, you'll get special days off on your anniversary day and birthday. The whole company is closed for two days in mid-August for summer holidays. Besides traditional Chinese holidays, the office is closed on Christmas Day.

Translation 譯文

（Steve Lee 將發現公司福利比他希望的還多。）

 Steve　我想這裡的規定不一樣吧？

 Ingrid　我很高興你提出這個問題，因為我們這裡採用彈性工時的制度，也就是說你可以選擇何時上班、何時下班。

 Steve　噢？我以為上班時間是朝九晚五。

 Ingrid　是的，但經理可以自己訂時間，你不必每天同時間開工，但你一定要在上午十點到下午三點的基本工時內出席。還有，你每週至少要工作 37 又 1/2 小時。

 Steve　了解，那無所謂，我比較好奇的是，公司每年都會幫我調薪嗎？

 Ingrid　會的。公司規定每年固定調一次薪。你的直屬主管會考核你的表現，據此向公司呈報該加多少薪給你。今年平均調薪的比例是 3%。

 Steve　我第一年有多少天的假？

 Ingrid　在今年剩下的時間裡，你有權休十天假。除此之外，在你的就職週年以及生日時還有特休。整個公司在八月中旬休息兩天放暑假，除了傳統三節假期外，公司在耶誕節也休息。

Words & Phrases 詞彙片語

- benefit 福利
- suspect 懷疑
- raise 提出；提起
- issue 問題
- adopt 採取；採納
- flex-time 彈性工時
- managerial 管理方面的；經理的
- core time （彈性工時制中的）基本工時
- put in 放進；投入
- at least 至少
- matter 要緊；重要
- curious 好奇的
- adjust 調整；調節
- immediate 直屬的
- supervisor 主管
- review 檢閱；批評
- compensation 報酬；賠償
- against 對照
- performance 績效；表現
- average 平均的
- hike 增加；提高
- be entitled to 有…的資格

- balance 剩餘部分；餘額
- in addition 此外
- anniversary day 就職週年紀念日

◀ A reminder 小提醒

> The office hours are 9:00 to 5:00.
>
> You're expected to put in at least 37 1/2 hours a week.
>
> This year the average hike is three percent.

以上是數字的寫法，一般英文報紙中，數字中只有 1～10（或 9）會拼出來（spell out），其他用阿拉伯數字表示，但若是學術論文等，則 1～99 的數字都會拼出來。但也有例外狀況，如在第一句中，即使 10 以下也會用數字表示，且百分比也多會拼出來，但在商業雜誌中，則多會使用 % 的符號及數字，如 35%。

✎ Exercise 練習

利用括弧中所提供的字來改寫句子：

❶ I thought the office hours were 9:00 to 5:00.

(was open, I was told, from)

❷ Managerial people can set their own work schedules.

(are allowed to choose, managers)

❸ You're expected to put in at least 37 1/2 hours a week.

(minimum of, work, supposed to)

Say It Differently 換種說法

Steve What about things like clean desks?

Ingrid There are no written rules about them, put you're expected not to leave anything on your desk when you leave the office for the day.

Steve You mean not even a calculator or a pencil case?

Ingrid You really should put them in your drawers. The desk top is supposed to be bare except for the telephone.

Steve Is that fairly well observed?

Ingrid Yes. Our management believes that a cluttered desk is a sign of a cluttered mind.

Translation 譯文

Steve 關於辦公桌清理的規定如何？

Ingrid 沒有明文規定，但我們希望在下班時不要留任何東西在桌上。

Steve 妳是說連計算機或鉛筆盒都不行？

Ingrid 你的確該把它們放在抽屜裡，桌面上除了電話外該是清空的。

Steve 大家都遵守嗎？

Ingrid 是的。管理階層相信雜亂的桌子是心思雜亂的象徵。

✱ written rule 明文規定

✱ for the day 一天（結束）

✱ calculator 計算機

✱ pencil case （鉛）筆盒

Unit 3

✳ drawer 抽屜

✳ bare 空的；赤裸裸的

✳ observe 遵守；觀察

✳ clutter 凌亂；雜亂

✳ sign 徵兆；跡象

Answer Key 練習解答

❶ I was told the office was open from 9:00 to 5:00.

❷ Managers are allowed to choose their own work schedules.

❸ You're supposed to work minimum of 37 1/2 hours a week.

Company Rules and Regulations

公司規章 (3)

◯ Sample Conversation 範文

(There's really such a thing as the Code of Ethics.)

 That sounds quite generous. What's the office regulation about lunch hours?

 It's supposed to be from 12 to 1, but people are somewhat flexible. You'll soon find out who keeps long lunch hours. But it's difficult to control the time precisely, especially if you're with a customer.

 Can I eat in?

Ingrid If you prefer to brown-bag it, you can eat in the cafeteria or the employees' lounge. Employees aren't allowed to use the conference room for eating. And you're not supposed to have noodles and things like that catered in. The cafeteria is open from 11 to 2 o'clock, and you can buy lunch ticket at Finance.

 I'll take the time to read the company rules and guidelines. But is there anything in particular I should pay attention to?

 As a sales manager, you may be in a position to be entertained or receive gifts from suppliers. We have strict regulations about excessive entertainment or presents. Customary seasonal gifts and occasional meal invitations are usually no problem, but you should watch out.

There's no such thing as a free lunch, as they say.

 Steve ＞ I know.

Translation 譯文

（的確有道德標準這玩意。）

 Steve ＞ 聽起來公司很大方。關於午餐時間，公司的規定為何？

Ingrid ＞ 午餐時間是從 12 點到 1 點，但大家都很有彈性，你很快會發現誰的午餐時間長，但要準確地控制時間很難，尤其是當你和客戶在一起時。

 Steve ＞ 我能在公司裡進餐嗎？

Ingrid ＞ 如果你喜歡自帶午餐，你可以在員工餐廳或員工休息室裡吃。員工不能在會議室裡吃東西，你也不可以在公司裡煮麵或類似的東西。員工餐廳從 11 點到 2 點開放，你可以到財務部買餐券。

 Steve ＞ 我會花時間讀公司規定和準則，但有沒有哪些規定我要特別注意的？

Ingrid ＞ 身為業務經理，你將會接受招待或收到供應商的禮物，對於過度的招待和禮品公司有嚴格的規定。習慣性的節令禮品以及偶爾的餐點招待通常不會有問題，但你要小心：就如俗語說的天下沒有白吃的午餐！

 Steve ＞ 我知道。

Words & Phrases 詞彙片語

 code of ethics 道德規範

somewhat 有些

precisely 精準地

- customer 客人;客戶
- eat in 內用 / 內食;在家吃飯
  take-out 外帶
- brown-bag 自帶午餐
- cafeteria (學校公司的) 自助食堂 / 餐廳
- lounge 休息室
- conference room 會議室
- noodles 麵條 (常用複數)
- catered in 外賣的
- finance 財務部
- in particular 特別的
- in a position of 能夠;可以
- entertain 招待;宴請
- supplier 供應商;業者
- excessive 過分的;過度的
- entertainment 娛樂;消遣;款待
- seasonal 節令的;當季的
- occasional 偶爾的;應景的
- invitation 邀約;邀請
- watch out 注意;小心
- free lunch 白吃的午餐;不勞而獲的事

Unit 3

A reminder 小提醒

一間公司本身會有很多規則以及關於不正當的金錢（bribery 賄賂、kick-back 回扣、embezzlement 挪用公款）或禮物收受等規定。

有些公司會要求全體成員一律穿西裝，只有在星期五才能穿著較休閒的服飾（dress-down Fridays）、吸菸、進食及其他種種內規，除了請教周遭的人之外，只有靠自己多觀察了！

現今推動的公交法（Fair Trade）以及個資法（Computer-processed Personal Data）的要求，個人薪資的計算和給付，休假請假的推定，還有許多不進公司從來沒聽過的規章規則和規定，這些對任何一位公司員工而言，其重要性絕不亞於專業知識和技能！

Exercise 練習

使用括弧中所提供的字來改寫句子：

❶ Employees are not allowed to use conference room for eating.

　(to eat in, employee rules, it's against)

❷ You may be in a position to receive gifts from suppliers.

　(vendors, presents, it's possible)

❸ Seasonal gifts and occasional meal invitations are no problem.

　(semi-yearly, dinner, all right)

❋ vendor 賣方；小販

❋ semi-yearly 年中的

Say It Differently 換種說法

 Steve If I had a business lunch with a customer, how should I charge that to the company?

 Ingrid Put it on your expense account sheet. You should describe where the business entertainment took place, who you entertained, what business relationship you have with the person, and what the purpose was.

 Steve Do I get a per diem for business trip?

 Ingrid As a matter of policy, you can opt either for a per diem or to get reimbursed for actual expense incurred.

Translation 譯文

 Steve 如果我和客戶吃午餐,我該如何把開銷記到公司帳上?

 Ingrid 記錄在你的費用單。你該寫明該項業務招待在哪裡舉行,對象是誰,你和那人的業務關係和目的為何。

 Steve 我在出差時有每日津貼嗎?

 Ingrid 基於政策,你可以選擇請領每日津貼或事後實支實銷。

* charge 將某項開支記載某人帳上
* expense account sheet 公務交際費的費用單
* describe 描述;說明
* take place 發生
* per diem 每日津貼
* as a matter of policy 政策上

✽ opt for 選擇

✽ get reimbursed for 得到 … 的償還

✽ incur 招致；引起

Answer Key 練習解答

❶ It's against employee rules to eat in the conference room.

❷ It's possible you may receive presents from vendors.

❸ Semi-yearly gifts and occasional dinner invitations are all right.

Talking on the Phone

電話交談 (1)

◯ Sample Conversation 範文

(An outside caller is trying to find someone.)

Marcy Good morning, Acme Company, Mr. Paul Jones's office.

Jack Calling for Paul Jones, please. My name is Yamamoto.

Marcy Sorry. I didn't catch your name.

Jack Yamamoto. Jack Yamamoto.

Marcy Would you spell that for me, sir?

Jack Sure. Y-A-M-A-M-O-T-O. Yamamoto.

Marcy Y-A-M-A-M-O-T-O?

Jack That's correct.

Marcy Will Mr. Jones know what this is in reference to?

Jack He should remember me from last week's trade symposium we attend together.

Marcy Mr. Jones's office.

Robert Is he in?

Marcy May I ask who's calling?

Robert I'm Robert Riddle.

Marcy Which company are you with, Mr. Little?

Robert No, my name is Riddle. R-I-double D-L-E. I work for Carpets Inter-

national. I wish to speak with Mr. Jones.

Marcy   One moment, please.

Translation 譯文

（來電尋人。）

Marcy   早安！極點公司，Paul Jones 辦公室。

Jack   我找 Paul Jones，我的名字是 Yamamoto。

Marcy   對不起，我沒聽清楚。

Jack   Yamamoto. Jack Yamamoto。

Marcy   先生，您能把字拼出來嗎？

Jack   可以，Y-A-M-A-M-O-T-O, Yamamoto。

Marcy   Y-A-M-A-M-O-T-O？

Jack   是的。

Marcy   您找 Jones 先生有什麼事嗎？

Jack   他應該記得我們上星期一起參加過貿易研討會。

Marcy   Paul Jones 辦公室。

Robert   他在位置上嗎？

Marcy   請問您大名是？

Robert   我叫 Robert Riddle。

Marcy   Little 先生，您在哪家公司服務？

Robert   不，我叫 Riddle，R-I- 兩個 D-L-E，我在國際地毯公司工作，我想和 Jones 先生談談。

Marcy   請稍等一會兒。

◯ Words & Phrases 詞彙片語

- 🗨 catch 聽見；聽清楚
- 🗨 spell 拼出來
- 🗨 in reference to 關於
- 🗨 symposium 討論會；座談會；論文集
- 🗨 attend 出席

  attend to 處理
- 🗨 carpet 地毯（若不是整片 wall-to-wall 或大片的則用 rug/area rug）

▌◀ A reminder 小提醒

早安（good morning）、午安（good afternoon）、日安（good day）或晚安（good evening/night），不論是接電話的問候或是面對面（face-to-face）的接觸，都是少不了的寒暄話。在英式英文中，上述的用語有時也會用在電話道別中，就好像「cheers」一樣。

如果是美式英語，道別的說法花樣就多了：

Have a nice day.

Enjoy your day.

Take care.

Have a good one.

Make it a good one.

Talk to you soon.

See you soon.

Catch you later.

I'll be in touch.

Exercise 練習

使用括弧中所提供的字來改寫句子：

1 Sorry. I didn't catch you name.

(recognize, pardon me)

2 Would you spell that for me, please?

(spelling, do you mind, your name)

3 Will Mr. Jones know what this is in reference to?

(is all about, does, understand)

Say It Differently 換種說法

 Frank This is Frank Muir. Is Steve Lee in?

 Nancy What did you say your name was?

 Frank Frank Muir.

 Nancy How do you spell it?

 Frank M-U-I-R. May I talk to Mr. Lee?

 Nancy What company are you with, Mr. Muir?

 Frank Muir & Kelly Associates.

 Nancy Is that a law firm?

 Frank Yes. Now, is he in today?

Translation 譯文

Frank 我是 Frank Muir，Steve Lee 在嗎？

Nancy 請重複一次您的大名好嗎？

Frank Frank Muir。

Nancy 請問您的名字怎麼拼？

Frank M-U-I-R，我能和 Lee 先生說話嗎？

Nancy Muir 先生，請問您在哪家公司任職？

Frank Muir 和 Kelly 事務所。

Nancy 是法律事務所嗎？

Frank 是的，嗯，他現在在嗎？

✱ associate 合夥人；同事

✱ law firm 法律事務所

✱ now 喂（表示轉變話題、要求、安慰、警告、解釋等）

Answer Key 練習解答

❶ Pardon me. I didn't recognize your name.

❷ Do you mind spelling your name for me, please?

❸ Does Mr. Jones understand what this is all about?

Talking on the Phone

電話交談 (2)

Sample Conversation 範文

(Mr. Jones is trying to get away from a call.)

Marcy (Using an extension) Mr. Jones, Mr. Riddle of Carpets International is on the line.

Paul Oh, he's bugging me again. Tell him I'm not interested to see him, not after he sold me that junk. Tell him to get lost!

Marcy I'm sorry, Mr. Riddle, Mr. Jones is not available right now. Would you mind calling back?

Robert What's the best time to call him?

Marcy I'm afraid he'll be completely tied up with oversea visitors this week.

Robert All right. I'll try again.

Marcy Thank you.

Paul Mike? This is a quickie since I have a department meeting starting in just a minute.

Mike What can I do for you, Paul?

Paul A question. Have you received the latest analysis of the new currency exchange policy?

Mike Yes, it just arrived this morning. You need a copy?

 Paul Yes. Could you send me a hard copy ASAP?

Translation 譯文

（Jones 先生不想接電話。）

Marcy （使用分機）Jones 先生，一位國際地毯公司的 Riddle 先生在線上。

Paul 噢，他又來煩我了。告訴他在他賣給我那件垃圾後，我不想再見他，
告訴他滾得遠遠地！

Marcy 很抱歉，Riddle 先生，Jones 先生現在沒空，你介不介意再打過來？

Robert 什麼時候打來找他最好？

Marcy 恐怕他這星期都會忙著接待國外客戶。

Robert 好吧，我會再打來。

Marcy 謝謝你。

Paul Mike？因為跨部門會議很快就要開始，有件急事請你幫忙。

Mike 我能為你做什麼嗎，Paul？

Paul 有個問題，你有沒有收到最新的新貨幣兌換政策的分析？

Mike 有的，今天早上剛到，你需要一份嗎？

Paul 是的，你能不能儘快送一份紙本給我？

Words & Phrases 詞彙片語

- extension 分機
- on the line 在線上
- bug 打擾；煩擾；折磨

- junk 垃圾；便宜貨；假貨
- get lost 滾開；迷路
- available 有空的；可以獲得的
- call back 回電；回收
- be tied up 有事；很忙；被占用的
- oversea 海外的
- quickie 迅速做完的事；急且短的事
- latest 最近的；最新的
- analysis 分析（複數：analyses）
- copy 一份；影本
- hard copy 紙本
- ASAP: (=as soon as possible) 儘快地

A reminder 小提醒

英文中形容詞／副詞，在做原級比較級和最高級變化時，一定要小心它的意思：

far – farther (與距離有關) – farthest

further (與程度有關) – furthest

old – older (與年紀有關) – oldest

elder (與輩分有關) – eldest

late – later (與時間有關) – latest

latter (與順序有關) – last

The small town is located farthest south of the city.

The issue (事件議題) needs further discussion.

My brother is older than I by five.

One should always respect the elders (長者).

I will see you later.

May and Jack are both capable (能幹的) workers; the former (前者) is good at (擅長) computer and the latter (後者) excels in (擅長) communication.

Exercise 練習

使用括弧中所提供的字來改寫句子：

① I'm sorry. Mr. Jones is not available right now.

(is occupied, I'm afraid, at the moment)

② What's the best time to call him?

(the most convenient, of the day, when's)

③ He'll be completely tied up with oversea visitors this week.

(out-of-town, he's busy)

✳ occupied 沒空；被占據的

✳ at the moment 現在

✳ convenient 方便的

Say It Differently 換種說法

Nancy Mr. Lee has someone with him. May I tell him what this is about?

Robert	Will you just have him call me back, please?
Nancy	Does he have your number, Mr. Muir?
Robert	Yes, he does.
Nancy	May I have it just in case?
Robert	It's (02)2545-5574.

Translation 譯文

Nancy	Lee 先生正在見客人，請問您找他有什麼事嗎？
Robert	你能請他回電給我嗎？
Nancy	Muir 先生，他有你電話嗎？
Robert	他有。
Nancy	能再給我以防萬一嗎？
Robert	(02)2545-5574。

✱ in case（以防）萬一

Answer Key 練習解答

❶ I'm afraid Mr. Jones is occupied at the moment.

❷ When's the most convenient time of the day to call him?

❸ He's busy with out-of-town visitors this week.

Talking on the Phone

電話交談 (3)

Sample Conversation 範文

(Steve Lee is talking to his colleague from the place he used to work.)

Dick > This is Dick Raw of Giant Plastics. How are you, Steve?

Steve > Hello, Dick. Well, this is a surprise. I haven't heard from you for ages. How have you been?

Dick > Oh, there have been ups and downs, but things are not too bad lately. Can you hear me clearly?

Steve > Barely. You sound as though you're speaking from the other side of the moon. Where are you calling from?

Dick > I'm in Hong Kong but I'll visit Taipei next week. Can we get together and catch up on each other and possibly do some business talks?

Steve > Of course. I never turn away an old friend. Let's see, I'll be out of town on Monday and Tuesday. Would Wednesday be all right?

Dick > That's super. What time would you say?

Steve > Well, the morning is pretty full. How about 3:30 p.m.? Or we could have lunch together.

Dick > I already have a lunch engagement on that day, so let's make it 4:30 p.m.. I'll come to your office.

Steve > Good. I look forward to seeing you then. Have a good trip over.

Dick Fine. Thank you. See you soon.

Steve Take care of yourself.

Dick You too, Steve.

Translation 譯文

（Steve Lee 正和他的老同事講電話。）

Dick 我是巨大塑膠的 Dick Raw，你好嗎，Steve？

Steve 真是意外啊，Dick。我好久沒聽到你的消息，最近如何？

Dick 有好有壞，但最近還不差，你聽得清楚嗎？

Steve 勉強。你聽起來好像是從月亮的另一邊打來，你從哪裡打的電話？

Dick 在香港，但我下星期將會去臺北，我們能不能聚聚，了解近況順便談些生意？

Steve 好啊！我絕不會拒絕老朋友。讓我想想，我星期一和二會外出，星期三如何？

Dick 棒極了，你說幾點？

Steve 早上行程都滿了，下午三點半如何？或者我們一起吃午餐。

Dick 我那天午餐已經有約，我們約下午四點半到你辦公室。

Steve 好，我很期盼看到你，來時一路順風！

Dick 好的，謝謝你，再見。

Steve 保重。

Dick 你也是，Steve。

Words & Phrases 詞彙片語

- colleague 同僚；同事
- used to 過去經常；(過去的) 習慣
- plastics 塑膠
- for ages 很長時間
- thing 事情；事態
- ups and downs 起伏盛衰
- barely 勉強；幾乎沒有
- as though 好像
- get together 聚一聚
- catch up 趕上
- turn away 拒絕；把臉轉過去
- out of town 出門；出城；不在城裡
- engagement 約會；訂婚；婚約
- make it 定（時間）

A reminder 小提醒

age 當「一輩子」或「時代」解釋，根據舊約聖經「詩篇」第 90 章第 10 節，人的一生可分成：

嬰兒（baby）：出生
幼兒（infant）：到 7 歲
兒童（child）：到 12 歲

Unit 4

青年（youth）：到 28 歲

壯年（manhood）：到 40 歲

中年（middle age）：到 65 歲

老年（old age）：以後 … ？

你現在是人生哪個階段呢？

另外，美式英文中誇張的用法是非常普遍的：

I am starved to death！(餓死了)

I am so starved I can eat a horse.

My back is killing me！(我的背痛死了)

I am dying for a cigarette！(想抽菸想死了)

誇張的詞藻、誇張的語調，再加上誇張的肢體動作，美式英文是種「演」出來的
語言！

✎ Exercise 練習

利用括弧中所提供的字來改寫句子：

❶ I haven't heard from you for ages.

(last, a long time, it's)

❷ You sound as though you're speaking from the moon.

(it sounds, calling, a far-off country)

❸ I'm in Hong Kong now but I'll visit Taipei next week.

(I'll leave, to visit Taipei)

✳ far-off 遙遠的

☼ Say It Differently 換種說法

Nancy Mr. Lee is in a meeting just now. I'll be glad to give him your message when he's free. What would you like me to tell him?

Dick Please tell him that Dick Raw called. My lunch appointment on Wednesday has been canceled. So I could have lunch with Steve if he's still available. Did you get that?

Nancy Yes, I did. I'll see if Mr. Lee could lunch with you on Wednesday. Where can I reach you, Mr. Raw?

Dick I'm staying at the Grand Hotel. Room 1234.

Nancy Thank you. I'll talk to Mr. Lee later and leave a message for you at the hotel this afternoon. Is that all right?

Dick Yes, that'd be excellent.

◗ Translation 譯文

Nancy Lee 先生正在開會，我很樂意在他有空時轉告他，你想要我告訴他什麼？

Dick 請告訴他 Dick Raw 來電，我星期三的午餐約會取消了。如果他仍有空，我可以和他一起吃午飯，妳記下來了嗎？

Nancy 是的，我記下來了。我會確認 Lee 先生是否能和你在星期三吃午飯，Raw 先生，我如何聯絡你呢？

Dick 我住在圓山飯店，1234 號房。

Unit 4

Nancy　謝謝你，我待會會告訴 Lee 先生，然後今天下午在你的住宿飯店留話，你覺得可以嗎？

Dick　可以，太棒了！

✳ message　消息；訊息

✳ cancel　取消

✳ get　記下來

✳ reach　與 … 取得聯繫

Answer Key 練習解答

❶ It's been a long time since I heard from you.

❷ It sounds like you're calling from a far-off country.

❸ I'll leave Hong Kong next week to visit Taipei.

 Visitor

訪客 (1)

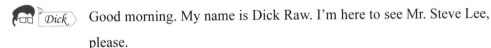 **Sample Conversation 範文**

(Dick Raw comes to the office to see Steve Lee.)

Dick Good morning. My name is Dick Raw. I'm here to see Mr. Steve Lee, please.

Receptionist Good morning, Mr. Raw. Is he expecting you?

Dick I have a lunch date with him.

Receptionist (On the phone) Miss Chen, this is the receptionist. I have a Mr. Raw here... Yes, I understand. Mr. Raw, please have a seat. Someone will be with you shortly.

Dick Thanks.

Steve Hello, Dick. It's so nice to see you again. You look very fit.

Dick Nice to see you, Steve. You look pretty healthy and prosperous yourself.

Steve Tell me what brings you to Taipei this time.

Dick I'll tell you what. The company is reassigning me here next month and I'm on a house-hunting trip.

Steve That's a marvelous news.

 Dick　Yes, but I'm a bit uneasy about apartment costs here. Will they be out of this world?

 Steve　No, on the contrary, they are quite affordable. I am sure your company will help you find a nice place. Let's go have a bite and hear the rest of your story.

Translation 譯文

（Dick Raw 來辦公室見 Steve Lee。）

 Dick　哈囉，我是 Dick Raw，我來見 Steve Lee 先生。

 Receptionist　早安，Raw 先生。他在等你嗎？

 Dick　我和他有午餐之約。

 Receptionist　（電話）Chen 小姐，我是接待員。有一位 Raw 先生…好的，我知道了。Raw 先生，請坐。馬上會有人來。

 Dick　謝謝。

 Steve　哈囉，Dick。看到你真好，你看起來身體狀況很好。

 Dick　Steve，很高興看到你，你看來也很健康和事事順心。

 Steve　告訴我是什麼風把你吹到臺北。

 Dick　讓我這麼說吧，公司下個月派我到臺北，我是來找房子的。

 Steve　那真是個好消息！

 Dick　是的，但是我對這裡的公寓開銷有點不安，它們是天價吧？

 Steve　不，剛好相反，一般人還算負擔得起。我確信你公司會幫你找個好地方，讓我們找個地方吃個飯，我要聽聽你的近況。

Words & Phrases　詞彙片語

- afar　從遠方
- receptionist　接待員
- expect　期待；預期
- date　約會；日期
- shortly　立即；馬上
- fit　強健的；身體狀況佳的
- prosperous　成功的；諸事順遂的
- I'll tell you what　你聽我說
- bring　促使
- reassign　分派；再分配
- house-hunting　找房子
- marvelous　好極了；不可思議的
- uneasy　不安的；不自在的
- apartment　公寓
- cost　花（費）
- on the contrary　相反地
- affordable　供得起的
- have a bite　吃點東西

A reminder 小提醒

在範文中有「I have a Mr. Raw here（有一位 Raw 先生）」的用法，有時在英文中，「some」也有這種功用：

> I have seen this movie in some movie theater.
>
> 我曾在某個電影院中看過這部電影。

照理說 some 通常都和複數名詞連用，若和單數名詞連用時，要譯成「某個」。

另外，專有名詞有時也有類似用法：

> There is an Edison in my office.
>
> 我辦公室裡有位（像愛迪生一樣的）發明家。

Exercise 練習

利用括弧中所提供的自來改寫句子：

❶ Tell me what brings you to Taipei this time.

　(what business, you have in, I'd like to know)

❷ The company is reassigning me here next month.

　(transferred to Taipei, being, shortly)

❸ I'm sure your company will help you find a nice place.

　(positive, employer, locate)

✱ would like to know 想知道

✱ transfer 調任

✱ positive 確信的

✱ employer 雇主

✱ locate 找到；找出

Say It Differently 換種說法

Steve How's the family doing?

Dick They're doing just fine. How's yours?

Steve My daughter is going off to college in the States this year. She hasn't decided which one, though. How's your business these days?

Dick You know, I've been heavily involved with the manufacturer of plastic food containers and I want to strengthen that business in Taipei.

Steve Uh-huh. Maybe we can do business together.

Dick Is there anyone at Acme Company that I can talk to?

Steve Yeah, I'll introduce him to you after lunch.

Translation 譯文

Steve 家裡近來都好吧？

Dick 他們都好，你的呢？

Steve 今年我女兒要到美國讀大學，她還沒決定去哪所，近來你的工作如何？

Dick 你是知道的，我和塑膠食品容器廠商的關係相當緊密，我想在臺北加強業務。

Steve 嗯，也許我們可以合作。

Dick 在極點公司裡有我能接洽的人嗎？

Steve 有，午餐後我會替你介紹。

✱ How's the family doing? 家庭近況如何？

✱ yours 你（的家庭）呢？

* go off to 動身前往

* States 美國

* though 但是

* be involved with 涉及某種活動

* manufacturer 製造商

* plastic container 塑膠容器

* strengthen 加強；鞏固

Answer Key 練習解答

❶ I'd like to know what business you have in Taipei this time.

❷ I'm being transferred to Taipei shortly.

❸ I'm positive your employer will help you locate a nice place.

Visitor

訪客 (2)

Sample Conversation 範文

(A mutual friend referred someone to Steve Lee.)

Nancy I just finished speaking with Mr. Doug Falcon of Champion Corp. He's been referred to us by Mel Johnson of Southern Fruits Co. Mr. Falcon said he's only in Taipei for a few days and he wanted to have an appointment to see you.

Steve Champion Corp. is a food company. I can't imagine what he wants out of us.

Nancy He said he'd like to see you tomorrow morning and visit our company.

Steve Tomorrow? I have a feeling it'll be a waste of time.

Nancy Since he got Mr. Johnson's introduction, maybe I could take him around for you.

Steve Good idea. Why don't you give him a tour first and then bring him in? But be sure to interrupt us after 15 minutes and remind me that I've got another meeting starting later on.

Nancy Yes, Mr. Lee.

Doug May I see Mr. Lee, please?

 Do you have an appointment with him?

 Of course, I do. I never drop in without an appointment.

 I beg your pardon. You must be Mr. Falcon. I do have a message from Mr. Lee's office to notify him as soon as you've arrived. His secretary will be here soon.

 Good morning, Mr. Falcon. My name is Miss Chen. I'm Mr. Lee's secretary. I'm sorry but Mr. Lee was called by the president about ten minutes ago. He should be back any minute now, but may I take you around the company first?

Translation 譯文

（共同朋友向 Steve Lee 引薦某人。）

 我剛和一位冠軍公司的 Doug Falcon 先生通完電話，他是南方水果公司的 Mel Johnson 先生介紹的。Falcon 先生說他只在臺北待幾天，所以他想要和你約時間見面。

 冠軍公司是食品公司，我不知道他想從我們這得到什麼。

 他說他想要明早和你見面並參觀公司。

 明天？我有種浪費時間的預感。

 因為他有 Johnson 先生的引薦，也許我能替你帶他參觀。

 好主意。妳何不先給他來個公司之旅接著再帶他來見我？但妳在 15 分鐘後一定要來中斷我們的談話，提醒我等會有另一個會議。

 是的，Lee 先生。

Doug　我能見 Lee 先生嗎？

 Receptionist　您和他有約嗎？

 Doug　當然，我絕不會不請自來的。

Receptionist　對不起。您一定是 Falcon 先生，Lee 先生的辦公室的確有留話，說您到了要通知他，他的祕書很快就會到這裡。

 Nancy　早安，Falcon 先生。我是 Lee 先生的祕書 Chen 小姐，很抱歉，Lee 先生十分鐘前才被董事長叫過去，他隨時都會回來，我能先帶您四處看看公司嗎？

Words & Phrases 詞彙片語

- mutual 互相的；共同的
- be referred to 介紹；推薦；提到
- imagine 想像
- a waste of time 浪費時間
- take...around 到各處
- tour 遊覽
- be sure to 務必
- interrupt 打斷
- remind 提醒
- later on 等會
- drop in 偶訪；突然造訪
- message 留言；信息
- notify 通知；報告

A reminder 小提醒

中英文之間的翻譯，有時會因語言使用的習性而不同：

introduce + 人 : 介紹

May I introduce my friend to you?

introduce + 物品 : 引進

The company is going to introduce a new product line (引進新系列產品)
to the public.

run:

The newspaper ran a story about the random killing on the MRT.

報紙報導捷運隨機殺人事件。

The young runs a store.

這個年輕人經營一家店。

The river runs through the small town.

這條河流經小城。

The old man hired a boy to run errands for him.

老人僱用小孩替他跑腿。

❋ Do the dishes 洗碗

❋ Take out the garbage 倒垃圾

❋ Make the bed 鋪床

❋ Eat one's soup 喝湯

❋ Take the medicine 服藥

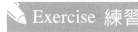 Exercise 練習

❶ I have a feeling it'll be a waste of time.

(can't help but feel, unproductive, meeting)

❷ Why don't you give him a tour first and then bring him in?

(Would you like to, bringing)

❸ Do you have an appointment with him?

(expecting, is he)

✱ can't help but 不得不

✱ unproductive 沒有結果的；沒生產力的

Say It Differently 換種說法

 Nancy　Mr. Falcon, would you like to take a look around our company first until Mr. Lee is available?

 Doug　I sure would.

Nancy　Come this way, please. Watch your step.

 Doug　What are these cartons?

Nancy　I believe they're for canned pineapples waiting for shipment.

 Doug　Where do you get your pineapples?

 Nancy　Mostly from the southern Taiwan. Let me take you to the packing area.

Translation 譯文

Nancy　Falcon 先生，在 Lee 先生有空前，您要不要先四處看看我們公司？

Doug　我當然要。

Nancy　請這邊來，走路小心。

Doug　這些紙箱是幹嘛的？

Nancy　我相信這些是要用來包裝待運的鳳梨罐頭。

Doug　你們從哪裡取得鳳梨的？

Nancy　大部分是來自南臺灣，讓我帶你到包裝區吧。

✱ Watch your step　留意腳下；走路小心

✱ carton　紙箱

✱ canned　罐裝的

✱ pineapple　鳳梨

✱ shipment　裝運

✱ packing area　包裝區

Answer Key 練習解答

❶ I can't help but feel it'll be an unproductive meeting.

❷ Would you like to give him a tour before bringing him in?

❸ Is he expecting you?

Visitor

訪客 (3)

Sample Conversation 範文

(Paul Jones and Steve Lee are conferring with an outside consultant.)

Jack > In conclusion, you may be pleased to know that the results of the market research by our firm are quite encouraging. Prospects are bright for the new weight-losing equipment to garner a substantial share of the market in a relatively short span of time.

Paul > Excellent. What's your projection for our market share a year after its launch?

Jack > If supported by a well-supported advertising campaign, it's quite possible to exceed 20 percent in the greater Taipei area. You'll find our detailed quantitative study in this report, which I'll leave with you.

Paul > That's very good, Mr. Blake. Any questions, Steve?

Steve > You still think it's a good strategy to focus on the greater Taipei?

Jack > Initially, yes. Our research shows that Acme Company has a strong quality image in the greater Taipei area and the up-market exercising equipment will capitalize on that.

Paul > This discussion has been very helpful and has cleared up most of our questions. We'll get to work on this right away.

Unit 5

Translation 譯文

（Paul Jones 和 Steve Lee 在和外部顧問開會。）

 Jack　總之，你應該會很高興知道我們公司的市場研究結果相當樂觀。減肥器材在短時間內可爭取到大量市場占有率，前景一片光明。

 Paul　好極了，你對新器材上市一年後我們市場占有率的預測為何？

 Jack　如果有良好廣告活動的支持，很可能在大臺北地區會超過 20%。你可以在這份留給你的報告中找到詳盡的數據。

 Paul　那很好，Blake 先生。Steve，還有問題嗎？

 Steve　你仍然覺得把重點放在大臺北地區是個好策略嗎？

 Jack　一開始是的，我們的研究顯示極點公司在大臺北地區有良好的品質形象，高檔健身器材將可利用那點。

 Paul　這是個很有幫助的討論，而且也對我們大部分問題做了澄清。我們馬上開始！

Words & Phrases 詞彙片語

● confer 商議；討論

● in conclusion 最後

● result 結果

● market 市場

● research 研究

● encouraging 鼓勵的；振奮的；振奮人心的

● prospect 可能性；前途

- weight-losing 減肥

- equipment 設備；器械

- garner 取得；獲得

- substantial 大量的；相當的

- share 市場占有率

- relatively 比較起來

- span（持續的）時間

- projection 推測

- launch 啟動；發動

- well-supported 良好支持的

- advertising campaign 廣告活動

- exceed 超越；超過

- greater Taipei area 大臺北地區

- detailed 詳盡的

- quantitative 量化的；數量的

- strategy 策略

- focus on 聚焦於；致力於

- image 形象

- up-market 高檔消費的

- capitalize on 充分利用 …

- clear up 解決（問題）

- work on 從事 … 工作

◀ A reminder 小提醒

「strategy」是「策略」，在經營管理上通常是指需長期經營的做法：

strategic planning（策略性規劃）
strategic alliance（策略性結盟）

「tactics」是「戰術；手段」，通常有短期運作的含意：

tactical advantage（戰術優勢）
tactical error（執行錯誤）

閱讀英文文章時，字面的解釋（literal meaning）往往未必能將完整的文意說出。所謂的「to read between the lines（在字裡行間找線索）」就變成理解和融會貫通時重要的關鍵！

✎ Exercise 練習

利用括弧中所提供的字來改寫句子：

❶ The results of the market research are quite encouraging.

(findings, reassuring)

❷ You'll find our detailed quantitative study in this report.

(take a look at, presented in)

❸ Our research shows that Acme Company has a strong quality image.

(your company, according to)

＊ findings　研究結果

＊ reassuring　可靠的；令人安心的

Say It Differently　換種說法

Paul　Mr. Blake, other than advertising, what do you recommend we do for the launch?

Jack　You may want to consider a kick-off press conference. You could also do a reception for representatives of the major fitness center chains.

Paul　I like press conference idea but I'm afraid we don't have much experience in that area.

Jack　I'll be happy to get you in contact with a couple of public relations firms that can organize a press conference for you.

Translation　譯文

Paul　Blake 先生，除了廣告外，你還建議我們為上市做些什麼？

Jack　你或許可以考慮召開上市記者招待會，你也可以為大型連鎖健身中心的代表辦個酒會。

Paul　我喜歡記者會的點子，但我們在那方面沒有經驗。

Jack　我很樂意替你聯絡幾個統籌記者會的公關公司。

＊ recommend　推薦；建議

＊ consider　考慮

＊ kick-off　開始（某事）

✱ press conference 記者招待會

✱ reception 茶會；酒會

✱ representative 代表

✱ major 主要的；較大的

✱ fitness center chain 連鎖健身中心

✱ get in contact with 和 … 交往 / 聯繫

✱ a couple of 兩個；幾個

✱ public relations firm 公關公司

✱ organize 安排；組織

Answer Key 練習解答

❶ The findings of the market research are quite reassuring.

❷ Take a look at our detailed quantitative study presented in this report.

❸ According to our research, your company has a strong quality image.

Preparation

出差在即

Sample Conversation 範文

(Steve Lee is talking to his boss about the coming trip.)

Paul〉 Hi, Steve. Getting ready for a vacation in the States?

Steve〉 Hello, Paul. It's no vacation. I've got to make a pitch for the management of Acme Company in New York and visit one production facility in Boston. And then...

Paul〉 I know, I know. I was only kidding. Are you excited?

Steve〉 I guess you could say so. I've been to New York but never to Boston.

Paul〉 The productions facility in Boston is so brand new that I haven't seen it either. I understand it has got all the leading-edge technologies. You'll also visit the main manufacturing plant in New Jersey?

Steve〉 Yes, I'll spend a couple of days there too. But what worries me is this presentation I have to give to the top management at Acme Company.

Paul〉 You're a worrier, aren't you? I'm positive that you'll come out of that meeting with flying colors. Give my regards to everybody. When will you be back?

Steve〉 Two weeks from Monday. I'll spend the last weekend in Hawaii on the way back. I have some friends there I haven't seen for a while.

Paul〉 Good. You deserve a vacation. Have a ball.

Translation 譯文

（Steve Lee 和他老闆討論即將到來的出差行程。）

 Paul 嗨，Steve。準備到美國去度假？

 Steve 哈囉，Paul。不是度假，我要到紐約為極點公司的高級主管做宣傳並去拜訪在波士頓的一個生產設施，接著…

 Paul 我知道，我知道。我只是在開玩笑，你感到興奮嗎？

 Steve 我想你可以如此說。我去過紐約但從沒去過波士頓。

 Paul 在波士頓的生產設施是如此的新穎連我都沒見過，我知道它有所有的頂尖技術，你也會去紐澤西州的主要製造工廠？

 Steve 是的，我將在那待一兩天。但讓我擔心的是對極點公司高階管理階層的簡報。

 Paul 你在杞人憂天吧？我肯定你會在簡報中表現出色的，替我向所有人問好。你何時回來？

 Steve 從星期一起兩週後，回來前最後一個週末我會待在夏威夷，我在那有些一陣子沒見面的朋友。

 Paul 好，你也該休個假了。好好玩！

Words & Phrases 詞彙片語

● States（口語）美國

● get ready for 準備妥當

● make a pitch for 為 … 做宣傳

● (top) management（高階）管理階層

- production facility 生產單位 / 設施
- kid 開玩笑
- brand new 嶄新的
- leading-edge 尖端的
- technologies 科技
- manufacturing plant 製造工廠
- presentation 簡報
- positive 確定；肯定
- come out 出現；表現
- with flying colors 出色的
- regard 致意；尊重
  give one's regard to 向 … 致意
- weekend 週末
  weekdays 週日
- deserve 應受報答；值得受賞
- have a ball 玩得高興

▌A reminder 小提醒

幽默（humor; being humorous）是在今天步調快速（fast-paced）的工商社會中唯一能讓上班族保持正常的萬靈丹（panacea, cure-all, silver bullet）！

但是能開他人玩笑（to play a joke on, to kid around）也要能讓他人開自己的玩笑，在許多的情況中，因為「只許州官放火不許百姓點燈（One may steal a horse, while another may not look over the hedge.）」的心態，使得很多人在自己成為他人消遣對象時，就會勃然大怒（to make one's blood boil），只有我自己才能開

自己的玩笑！

在熙來攘往的日子裡，給他人些歡笑，給自己點歡笑。

就算出醜（make a fool of oneself）又何妨？

Exercise 練習

利用括弧中所提供的字來改寫句子：

❶ The manufacture facility is so brand new that I haven't seen it either.

(just opened, so, visited)

❷ What worries me is this presentation I have to give to the top management at Acme.

(I'm worried about, in New York)

❸ I'll spend the last weekend in Hawaii on the way back.

(en route to Hawaii, intend to)

✳ en route 在途中

✳ intend to 想要，打算

Say It Differently 換種說法

 Paul Have you put together the business presentation?

 Steve Yes, and I'll be using a dozen overhead slides too. But frankly I feel a bit edgy about it. Am I supposed to tell a joke before I start?

 Paul No, don't do that if you're not comfortable with it. Just rehearse well and be prepared to field some tough questions. I know you've put a lot of hours into it. You'll come out all right.

 Steve I certainly hope so.

Translation 譯文

 Paul 你把業務簡報弄好了嗎？

 Steve 是的，我也將要用 12 張左右的投影片。但老實說我覺得有些焦慮，我該在開始前說個笑話嗎？

 Paul 不要，除非你覺得自在否則不要。只要好好練習並準備好回答些棘手的問題，我知道你在簡報上投入很多時間，你會勝出的。

 Steve 我真的希望如此。

* put together 組合；拼裝起來
* dozen 一打
* overhead slides 投影片
  transparency 幻燈片
* edgy 急躁的；焦慮的
* frankly 坦白地
* comfortable 舒適的；自在的
* rehearse 排練；排演
* field （巧妙地）回答
* tough 棘手的；困難的
* come out 結果是

Answer Key 練習解答

① The manufacture facility just opened, so I haven't visited it either.

② I'm worried about this presentation I have to give in New York.

③ I intend to spend the last weekend in Hawaii en route to Taipei.

Tie up Loose Ends

行前交代

Sample Conversation 範文

(Steve Lee is making sure all things are taken care of.)

 Steve I'll pick up my traveler's check after lunch and go straight to the ad agency to look at the final proof of the new ad series. I'll be back around 4, but I'm going to be tied up for the rest of the day. Say, Nancy, who am I having lunch with today?

 Nancy Mr. Jennings of the Marketing Association.

 Steve Oh, that's right. By the way, I have a notice here from the seminar committee about next week's meeting. Could you call the Chamber of Commerce and say that I won't be able to make it?

 Nancy Yes, I will. There are a couple of phone messages, none urgent. And here's your memo on competitors' move in Taiwan that I've prepared in rough draft.

 Steve This looks great. You know something, Nancy? You are a fantastic secretary. As always, you've caught my spelling and grammatical errors and corrected them. I don't know what I'd do without you.

 Nancy Thanks. That's what I really want – compliments rather than a raise.

Steve You bet.

Translation 譯文

（Steve Lee 確定所有事都處理妥當。）

Steve 我午餐後會去拿我的旅行支票並直接去廣告公司看新廣告系列的完稿。
我將在四點回來，但我今天都會很忙。對了，Nancy，我要和誰吃午
餐啊？

Nancy 行銷協會的 Jennings 先生。

Steve 對噢，順便一提，我有份研討委員會關於下星期會議的通知。妳能不
能告訴商會我無法參加？

Nancy 是的，我會。有幾個電話留言，沒有緊急的。這是你對競爭對手在臺
策略備忘錄的草稿。

Steve 看來不錯，Nancy，你知道嗎？妳是位很棒的祕書，就和以往一樣，
妳抓到我拼字和文法的錯誤並予以更正，沒有妳我不知要如何是好。

Nancy 謝了，這正是我要的：讚美而非加薪。

Steve 不客氣！

Words & Phrases 詞彙片語

- tie up loose ends 處理枝節；收尾
- pick up 拿；拾起；接載；接機；逮捕
- traveler's check 旅行支票
- go straight to 直接去
- ad agency 廣告公司
- final proof 終校樣張

- ad series　廣告系列；廣告輯
- be tied up　很忙
- rest　剩餘部分；休息
- marketing association　行銷協會
- by the way　順帶一提
- notice　通知；通告
- seminar　研討會
- committee　委員會；籌備會
- Chamber of Commerce　商會
- make it　及時趕到；成功
- message　留言；訊息
- urgent　緊急的
- memo: (= memorandum)　備忘錄
- competitor　競爭對手
- rough draft　草稿
- You know something?　你知道嗎？
- fantastic　極好的；奇妙的
- as always　一如往昔
- spelling　拼字
- error　錯誤
- compliment　恭維；讚美
- raise　加薪
- You bet!　的確；當然

A reminder 小提醒

本段範文的結尾中，祕書 Nancy 說：「只要讚美不要加薪」這是反話！而她老闆也就順水推舟（go with the flow）用「那是當然」來回答。在歐美國家公司上班，員工最盼望的就是實質的獎勵（substantial rewards）：獎金（bonus）、公司付費的休假（paid vacation），甚至於汽車（automobile），往往會比讚美或是鼓勵（a word of encouragement/a pat on the shoulder）來的更具吸引力！

當然，絕非所有的人都是物質至上，有時「禮輕情意重（What counts is the thoughts！）」，身為上司老闆的人也實在不該太過吝嗇小氣（stingy, miserly, tight-fisted），畢竟不快樂的員工就不可能有好的表現，而表現不好的員工又怎能替公司賺錢呢？

Exercise 練習

利用括弧中所提供的字來改寫句子：

❶ Could you call them and say I won't be able to make it?

(will be absent, give them a ring, advise)

❷ You've caught my grammatical errors and corrected them.

(were good enough to, mistakes, correct)

❸ I don't know what I'd do without you.

(be helpless, your assistance)

✱ absent 缺席

✱ give someone a ring 打電話給 …

✱ advise 通知

* good enough to 好到足以 …
* assistance 協助

Say It Differently 換種說法

Nancy Steve, I've listed on this sheet your passport number and the numbers on your credit cards and traveler's checks.

Steve What would I need that for?

Nancy In case you lose your cards or passport, the list should come in handy.

Steve Well, I hope that won't happen but thanks all the same.

Nancy You should watch out in New York. I've heard so many horror stories.

Steve Those stories tend to exaggerate. Don't worry.

Translation 譯文

Nancy Steve，我在這張紙上列出了你的護照、信用卡，還有旅行支票的號碼。

Steve 我要它們幹嘛？

Nancy 萬一你遺失的信用卡或護照，這張紙該能派上用場。

Steve 好吧！我希望那別發生，不過還是謝謝妳。

Nancy 你在紐約要小心，我聽過很多恐怖的故事。

Steve 那些故事都過於誇大，別擔心！

* list 列出
* credit card 信用卡
* What would I need that for? 要它幹嘛？

✱ in case 萬一

✱ come in handy 遲早有用

✱ horror 恐怖

✱ tend to 有…的傾向

✱ exaggerate 誇張

Answer Key 練習解答

❶ Could you give them a ring and advise them I will be absent?

❷ You were good enough to catch my grammatical mistakes and correct them.

❸ I'd be helpless without your assistance.

Can You Do Me a Favor?

能幫個忙嗎？

Sample Conversation 範文

(Steve Lee is lending a helping hand.)

Steve Now do you have a copy of my itinerary?

Nancy Yes.

Steve You know where to get in contact with me. I'll leave the address of my friends in Hawaii in case you have to reach me there. You can open all my letters except for the ones marked "Personal." All invoices can wait until I come back, I think. I'll initial these interoffice memos now. Incidentally, is there anything you want me to get you in the States?

Nancy That's very kind of you, Steve. But no thanks. Instead, I wonder if you can do a small favor for me while you're in the New York area.

Steve What is it?

Nancy My brother works there. Would you be good enough to give him some pictures and tell him I'm doing all right? Here's his number.

Steve I'll be delighted to. I'll tell him how well you're doing and all the rest of it. Anything you want me to take to him? No? Now can you do me a small favor in return while I'm away?

Nancy Of course.

Unit 6

 Steve Can you water my plants and take good care of them?

Nancy Sure. I'll talk to them every morning like you do.

Translation 譯文

（Steve Lee 義伸援手。）

 Steve 你有我行程的影本嗎？

Nancy 有的。

 Steve 妳知道在哪裡和我聯絡。萬一妳必須找到我，我會把我夏威夷朋友的住址給妳。除了註明私人外，妳可以拆我的信。我想所有發票都可以等到我回來。我現在要簽署內部簽呈。對了，有沒有任何東西我能從美國帶回來給妳的？

 Nancy 你真是好心，Steve。但我沒有，謝謝你。不過，我不知道你在紐約時能否幫我個小忙。

Steve 什麼事？

 Nancy 我兄弟在那工作。你能不能幫個忙給他一些照片並告訴他我很好？這是他的電話號碼。

 Steve 我很樂意做，我會告訴他妳近況很好還有其他的。有沒有任何要帶給他的東西？沒有嗎？那妳能在我不在時幫我個小忙嗎？

Nancy 沒問題。

 Steve 妳能替我的植物澆水並好好照顧它們嗎？

Nancy 當然，我每天早上都會和你一樣和它們說話。

Words & Phrases 詞彙片語

- copy 本；份；冊
- itinerary 旅行；計畫；行程表
- get in contact with 與 … 聯絡
- except for 除了 … 外
- personal 私人郵件（有時也會標示為 personal and confidential 機密）
- invoice 發票
- interoffice memo 公司內部通報字條
- incidentally 順便一提
- That's very kind of you 你真好
- wonder 想知道；不知道
- do ... a favor 幫忙；做好事
- doing all right 還不錯
- be delighted to 很高興；很樂意 …
- in return 回報；交換
- water (V.) 澆水
- plant 植物

A reminder 小提醒

「bring」「take」「get」和「carry」要如何區分呢？

對以英文為母語的人而言，上述各字的使用多為習慣。外國人用時都是視為理所

當然（take it for granted）！但對學習英文的人而言，雖然四字意思相當，但所指

方向不同：

bring：把人事物帶到說話人的所在地

Bring me some water, please.

take：把人事物從說話人的所在地帶到別處

Take the box to my room.

get：從說話人的所在地到別處取回人事物

Can you get the children this afternoon?

carry：泛指隨身攜帶

Be sure to carry your ID all the time.

另外，請人幫忙時多用：

Can you give me a hand?

Can you help me?

使用「favor」時一定要記住：恩惠是要還的！

I did you a favor last time, now it's time to return my favor.

Exercise 練習

利用括弧中所提供的字來改寫句子：

❶ You know where to get in contact with me.

(reach, how to)

❷ All invoices can wait until I come back, I think.

(guess you can, until)

❸ That's very kind of you, Steve. But no thanks.

(a sweet person, that's all right)

✳ reach（透過電話）聯絡
✳ sweet 親切的；溫柔的

☼ Say It Differently 換種說法

Steve Are the airline tickets here too?

Nancy No, the travel agency said they'll send them to us this afternoon by messenger. They'll also bring your travel insurance cards.

Steve Good. Have you been able to confirm my hotel for one night in Hawaii?

Nancy Not yet, but I'll fax the name of the hotel via the Acme Company as soon as confirmation is received.

◑ Translation 譯文

Steve 機票也在這嗎？

Nancy 不，旅行社說他們今天下午會派人送給我們。他們也會帶來你的旅行保險卡。

Steve 好，妳是否已幫我確定在夏威夷住宿一晚的旅館？

Nancy 還沒，但確定後，我會儘快透過極點公司把旅館名字傳真給你。

✳ ticket 票；入場券；交通違規罰單
✳ travel agency 旅行社

* insurance card 保險卡

* confirm (V.) 確認

* not yet 還沒；尚未

* via 經由

* confirmation (N.) 確認；證實；批准

Answer Key 練習解答

❶ You know how to reach me.

❷ I guess you can hold all invoice until I come back.

❸ You are a sweet person, Steve. But that's all right.

Things Could Have Been Worse!

事情可能會更糟！

🔊 Sample Conversation 範文

(Steve Lee is talking to Eric Turner of Acme Company about how he started off the day on the wrong foot.)

 Eric Welcome to the Big Apple. How was your flight?

 Steve The flight was very smooth but I received a most unusual welcome yesterday.

 Eric What happened?

 Steve I'd just arrived at JFK. I went to a newsstand to buy a newspaper and put down my shoulder bag to pay for it. I counted the change and looked at where I'd put the bag. It was gone. It was just a matter of a few seconds.

 Eric Oh, it sounds like you were ripped off. Real pros need only that much time to do the job. I am very sorry to hear that.

 Steve I should have been more careful. I felt bad.

 Eric Did you contact the police?

 Steve Yes. I was told that I was the sixth traveler to report trouble at the airport yesterday. New York thieves have a field day.

 Eric What was in the bag?

Steve Traveler's check for $1,000, some credit cards, and my return airplane ticket. Luckily, I carried about $200 in my hip pocket, so that was safe at least.

Eric It's ironic, because that's usually the most dangerous spot to carry cash.

Translation 譯文

（Steve Lee 正在和極點公司的 Eric Turner 述說自己一開始就不順的一天。）

Eric 歡迎來到大蘋果，飛行一路上如何？

Steve 飛行還平順但昨天我受到最不尋常的歡迎式。

Eric 怎麼了？

Steve 我剛到達甘迺迪機場，我去書報攤買報紙並把我的肩袋放下付錢。我算錢時看我放袋子的地方，不過短短幾秒鐘，袋子不見了。

Eric 看來你被偷了，真的高手只要那點時間就能到手。我很遺憾聽到這件事。

Steve 我應該更小心，我覺得不舒服。

Eric 你報警了嗎？

Steve 有，他們告訴我是昨天第六個在機場遇到麻煩的旅客。紐約的小偷們昨天過得很愉快！

Eric 袋子裡有什麼？

Steve 價值一千美元的旅行支票，一些信用卡，還有我的回程機票。幸運地是我在褲子的後口袋裡放了 200 美元，至少那些錢是安全的。

Eric 有點諷刺，因為那裡通常是放錢最危險的地方。

Words & Phrases 詞彙片語

- to start off on the wrong foot 不好的開始
- the Big Apple 紐約市
- flight 飛行；飛機；航班
- smooth 平穩的；平滑的
- receive 遭到；收到
- unusual 不平常的；奇特的
- newsstand 書報攤
- shoulder bag 肩袋
- change 零錢
- a matter of 大約
- rip off 偷竊；搶劫
- pro 專家
- have a field day 非常愉快
- hip pocket 臀袋；褲子後口袋
- ironic 諷刺的
- spot 地方；地點
- cash 現金

A reminder 小提醒

「I should have been more careful.」中用的 should + have + p.p. 是與事實相反的假設語氣中常見的句型：

should + have + p.p.: 該做未做

I should have exercised more when I had the chance.

would + have + p.p.: 會做未做

I would have come if I had time then.

could + have + p.p.: 能 (力) 做未做

I could have helped you with the moving if I had time.

might + have + p.p.: (可) 能做未做

I might have made some terrible mistakes when I was little.

must + have + p.p.: (根據證據) 一定是 …

It must have rained last night for the ground was wet this morning.

Exercise 練習

利用括弧中所提供的字來改寫句子：

❶ The flight was very smooth but I received a most unusual welcome.

(bizarre, encounter, pleasant)

❷ Real pros need only that much time to do the job.

(professional thieves, just a few seconds)

❸ I was told that I was the sixth traveler to report trouble.

(police said, get into, visitor from oversea)

✷ bizarre 奇怪的；奇特的；匪夷所思的

✷ encounter 遭遇（危險）；遇到（人）

✷ pleasant 令人愉快的；舒適的

✻ professional 職業的；專業的

✻ get into 陷入

Say It Differently 換種說法

Eric〉 It must have been a professional thief to do such a quick job.

Steve〉 That's what the police told me too.

Eric〉 Were they helpful to you?

Steve〉 Not really. They just had me file a report. I guess they're too busy with more serious crimes.

Eric〉 I understand that foreign travelers are often victimized abroad, because they believe in carrying cash around, don't they?

Steve〉 That's true. But I've learned my lesson now.

Translation 譯文

Eric〉 一定是個專業的小偷才能下手如此快。

Steve〉 那正是警察告訴我的。

Eric〉 他們對你有所幫助嗎？

Steve〉 並沒有，他們只把我的報告歸檔。我猜他們因更嚴重的犯罪而太忙了。

Eric〉 我知道外國旅客因為深信隨身攜帶現金而常在海外受害，不是嗎？

Steve〉 這倒是真的，但我學到經驗了。

✻ quick 快速的

✻ helpful 有幫助的

* file 提出；歸檔

* serious 嚴重的；嚴肅的

* crime 犯罪

* victimized 不當地使某人受害；欺負某人

* carry... around 隨身攜帶

* learn one's lesson 學到經驗

Answer Key 練習解答

❶ The flight was very pleasant but I had a most bizarre encounter.

❷ Professional thieves need just a few seconds to do the job.

❸ Police said that I was the sixth visitor from oversea to get into trouble.

 Casual Exchanges during a Conference

言不及義！？

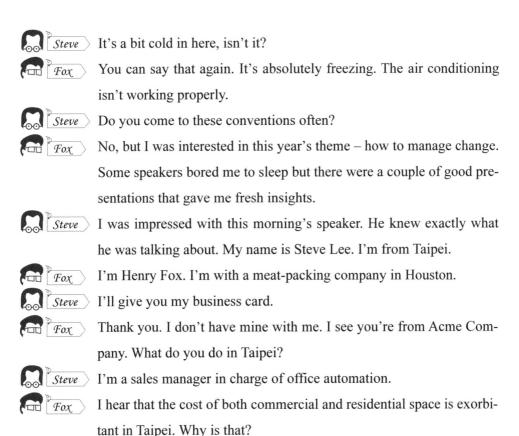

🔘 Sample Conversation 範文

(Steve Lee is talking to someone while taking part in a convention.)

Steve It's a bit cold in here, isn't it?

Fox You can say that again. It's absolutely freezing. The air conditioning isn't working properly.

Steve Do you come to these conventions often?

Fox No, but I was interested in this year's theme – how to manage change. Some speakers bored me to sleep but there were a couple of good presentations that gave me fresh insights.

Steve I was impressed with this morning's speaker. He knew exactly what he was talking about. My name is Steve Lee. I'm from Taipei.

Fox I'm Henry Fox. I'm with a meat-packing company in Houston.

Steve I'll give you my business card.

Fox Thank you. I don't have mine with me. I see you're from Acme Company. What do you do in Taipei?

Steve I'm a sales manager in charge of office automation.

Fox I hear that the cost of both commercial and residential space is exorbitant in Taipei. Why is that?

Steve With limited space available, it's hard to slash down the rental cost.

Translation 譯文

（Steve Lee 在參加會議時和他人交談。）

Steve　這裡有點冷，不是嗎？

Fox　你還真的說對了，真是冷颼颼的。空調有問題。

Steve　你常來參加這些會議嗎？

Fox　不，但我對今年如何「應對變化」的主題感興趣，一些講者讓我想入睡，但有幾個是讓我有新領悟的好講座。

Steve　今早的講者讓我印象深刻，他知道自己所講的內容是什麼。我是 Steve Lee，我來自臺北。

Fox　我是 Henry Fox，我在休士頓一家肉類包裝公司工作。

Steve　這是我的名片。

Fox　謝謝你，我身邊沒帶名片。我知道你是極點公司的人，你在臺北負責的業務是？

Steve　我是負責辦公室自動化的業務經理。

Fox　我聽說臺北商辦和住宅要價都非常高昂，為什麼呢？

Steve　有限的空間讓租金很難下降。

Words & Phrases 詞彙片語

● conference 討論會

● convention 會議；（政黨，組織）大會

● a bit 有一點

● You can say that again 我同意你的意見

- absolutely 完全地；絕對地
- freezing 極冷的
- theme 主題
- bore 令人厭煩
- a couple of 兩個；幾個
- fresh 清新的；新鮮的
- insight 洞察力；領悟
- be impressed with 留下深刻印象
- exactly 確切地；完全地
- meat-packing 肉類包裝
- business card 名片
- mine: (= my + N.) 我的 …
- in charge of 負責；主其事
- office automation 辦公室自動化
- cost 成本；開銷
- commercial 商業的
  commercials 廣告
- residential 住宅的
- space 空間
- exorbitant （要求，收費）過高的
- available 可利用的

A reminder 小提醒

在社交場合中如何「破冰」打破僵局，是件相當重要的事。天氣、運動、節慶活

動及其他非私人性的話題，都能發揮功用（do the trick）！

但某些如宗教信仰或政治議題相關的討論，除非彼此有共識，否則會適得其反（back fire）。私人相關的議題，如：婚姻狀況或工作收入更是閒談時要避免的忌諱（taboo），有時問對方結婚與否能被接受，但千萬別問為何不婚！可以問有幾個小孩，但千萬別問為何不生小孩。

名片是讓對方記得自己及讓自己建立人脈（connections）的好工具，把自己在不同場合中所得到的名片，分門別類地整理好，日後會是自己非常有用的索引資料。

Exercise 練習

利用括弧中所提供的字來改寫句子：

❶ Some speakers bored me to sleep.

　(were so boring that, put me)

❷ I see you're from ABC Trading Company.

　(with, your card says)

❸ Companies depend to a large extent on the limited space.

　(greatly dependent on)

Say It Differently 換種說法

 Fox ⟩ You folks are really good at manufacturing computer hardware, don't you?

 Steve ⟩ I guess you can say that, though, we are trying hard to switch from OEM to OBM, but that takes time.

 Fox ⟩ I'd like to visit Taiwan sometimes; not necessarily for business.

Steve ⟩ Give me a call if you do visit Taiwan in the future. There are a lot to meet the eye!

 Fox ⟩ Don't mind if I do.

Translation 譯文

 Fox ⟩ 你們臺灣人很擅長製造電腦硬體，對吧？

 Steve ⟩ 我想你可以如此說，儘管我們很努力地從代工轉換到自創品牌，但那要花時間。

 Fox ⟩ 我希望哪天去拜訪臺灣，不一定是公事。

 Steve ⟩ 將來到臺灣時打電話給我，有很多值得一看的。

 Fox ⟩ 如果我真的打，你可別介意！

* good at 擅長
* hardware 硬體
* switch 轉換
* OEM: (Original Equipment Manufacturing) 代工
* OBM: (Original Brand Manufacturing) 自創品牌
* take time 花時間
* to meet the eye 滿足眼睛；可看

Answer Key 練習解答

❶ Some speakers were so boring that they put me to sleep.

❷ Your card says you're with ABC Trading Company.

❸ Companies are greatly dependent on the limited space.

The Small Talks Continue

說不完了！

Sample Conversation 範文

(Steve Lee is having a conversation with Eric Tuner.)

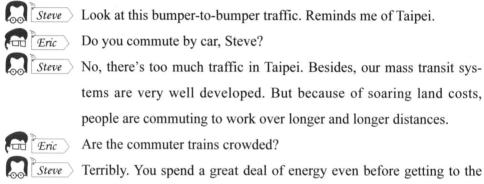

Steve Look at this bumper-to-bumper traffic. Reminds me of Taipei.

Eric Do you commute by car, Steve?

Steve No, there's too much traffic in Taipei. Besides, our mass transit systems are very well developed. But because of soaring land costs, people are commuting to work over longer and longer distances.

Eric Are the commuter trains crowded?

Steve Terribly. You spend a great deal of energy even before getting to the office. I change trains at Taipei Main Train Station, where over hundreds and thousands of passengers get on and off trains each day.

Eric That's a lot! What about housing? Did you own any houses?

Steve Yes, but it's very small. In fact, it's so small that we have to use condensed milk and concentrated juice!

Eric You've got to be kidding! Is housing expensive in Taipei?

Steve "Astronomical" is the word. I live about an hour away from downtown Taipei. Even there a piece of land about the size of my handkerchief costs more than a couple of thousand dollars.

Translation 譯文

（Steve Lee 在和 Eric Turner 說話。）

Steve　看看這車水馬龍的盛況，讓我想到臺北。

Eric　Steve，你開車上班嗎？

Steve　不，臺北交通太擠了。除此之外，我們的大眾運輸系統發展地很完備，
但因高漲的土地成本，大家都從越來越遠的地方通勤上班。

Eric　通勤火車擁擠嗎？

Steve　非常擠，你在到辦公室前就耗掉不少力氣。我在臺北車站換車，在那
裡有成千上萬的乘客上下車。

Eric　那真是很多！房子怎樣？你自己擁有房子嗎？

Steve　有，但很小。實際上，它小到我們必須用濃縮牛奶（煉乳）和濃縮果
汁！

Eric　你說笑了！在臺北住屋貴嗎？

Steve　「天文數字」該是正確的字。我住在離臺北市中心一小時距離的地方，
就算在那裡像我手帕大小的土地也要花個一兩千塊錢。

Words & Phrases 詞彙片語

- bumper-to-bumper traffic　一輛車接一輛車的交通（擁塞）；車水馬龍
- remind + 人 +of　提醒某人某事
- mass transit system　大眾運輸系統
- well developed　發展完備地
- soaring　高聳的；沖天的

- cost 費用；成本
- commute 通勤
- distance 距離
- commuter train 通勤列／火車；市郊往返列車
- energy 精力；精神；能源
- hundreds and thousands of 數以千計的
- passenger 乘客
- own 擁有
- housing 住屋、房舍供給
- condensed milk 煉乳
- concentrated juice 濃縮果汁
- astronomical 天文的；龐大的
- handkerchief 手帕

▌A reminder 小提醒

「condensed milk」和「concentrated juice」煉乳和濃縮果汁，是典型的美式幽默。利用濃縮來形容房子的小，美國文化中的反諷和自我解嘲往往可以在言語中略見一二：

She is vertically challenged.

她很矮。

（vertically: 垂直地；直立地）

Where can I dump these white elephants?

這些無用的東西丟到哪裡？

（white elephant: 大而無當的東西）

一語雙關（pun）在解讀美式英語時是個很重要的技巧，如果字字都以字面意思（literal meaning）為主，你會發現你不僅聽不懂更會笑不出來！

Exercise 練習

利用括弧中所提供的字來改寫句子：

❶ Because of soaring land costs, people are commuting to work over longer and longer distances.

(increasingly long, are forcing people)

❷ You spend a great deal of energy even before you get to the office.

(by the time you get to, already spent)

❸ Is housing expensive in Taipei?

(housing costs, high)

✱ increasingly 漸增地；越來越多地

✱ force 強迫；逼迫

✱ by the time 到 … 的時候

Say It Differently 換種說法

 Eric > Why is housing so expensive?

 Steve > The supply of land for residential use is very scarce. And there's a tremendous concentration of population around major cities.

 Eric > What's homeownership like?

 Steve > It's around 60 percent.

 Eric　That's not too bad, is it?

 Steve　No, the only thing is the Taiwanese homes are so much smaller. The average house built in Taiwan is only half the size of a new American home.

Translation 譯文

 Eric　為何房屋如此貴？

 Steve　住宅用地的供給非常稀少，而在主要城市周遭又有大量的人口聚居。

 Eric　住屋擁有率是多少？

 Steve　大概六成。

 Eric　並不壞，對吧？

 Steve　是不壞，只不過臺灣房子要小多了。一般臺灣房屋大小只有美國新屋的一半。

＊ supply　供給

＊ residential use　住宅（用地）

＊ scarce　稀少的；罕見的

＊ tremendous　巨大的；極度的

＊ concentration　集中

＊ major　主要的

＊ homeownership　房屋擁有率

＊ average　平均的；一般的

Answer Key 練習解答

❶ Soaring land costs are forcing people to commute to work over increasingly long distance.

❷ You've already spent a great deal of energy by the time you get to the office.

❸ Are housing costs high in Taiwan?

The Way of Tipping

小費之道 (1)

Sample Conversation 範文

(Steve Lee tries to find out to tip or not to tip.)

 Steve　Thank you, Eric. That was the most magnificent meal I've had in years. You'll have to let me reciprocate the next time you're in Taipei.

 Eric　Don't worry about it, Steve. That's not a big deal, though, because I know that a steak dinner would cost at least three times as much in Taipei. Just excuse me for a second while I check the numbers here and figure out how much to give the waiter. Hmm, by the way, what do you do about tipping in Taipei?

 Steve　We don't.

 Eric　No tipping? Now that's what I call a civilized system.

 Steve　At hotels and some restaurant they add a service charge to the bill, but other than that, tipping isn't customary.

 Eric　What about cab drivers and porters?

 Steve　In a cab you pay what it says on the meter. I generally tip hotel porters, but in some first-class hotels they're instructed not to accept gratuities.

 Eric　You'd have a revolution on your hands if you tried to introduce that sort of system here.

Steve It's a big difference between Taiwanese and American customers. It created complications, I've noticed, at Chinese restaurants here in the States. A Dim Sum place I went to last I was here had a big sign in Chinese saying, "You are requested to tip here." I guess people feel so at home that they tend to leave without tipping.

Translation 譯文

（Steve Lee 想知道該付還是不該付小費。）

Steve 謝謝你，Eric。那是我多年來最豐盛的一頓飯，下回你來臺北時一定要讓我回請你。

Eric Steve，別放在心上，沒什麼大不了的。因為我知道一頓牛排餐在臺北會要花上三倍價錢。先失陪一下，我要對對數字並算算給服務生的小費。嗯，對了，你們在臺北小費是怎麼給的？

Steve 我們不給。

Eric 不給小費？那才是我所謂的文明制度。

Steve 有些旅館、餐廳會在帳單上加上服務費，但除此之外，習慣上不給小費。

Eric 那計程車駕駛和搬行李的人呢？

Steve 你只付在計程車里程錶上顯示的金額。我通常會給旅館行李員小費，但在一些一流旅館，他們受的訓練是不接受小費。

Eric 如果在這裡引入那種制度，馬上就會鬧革命了。

Steve 臺灣和美國客人大不相同。我注意到這讓美國的中式餐廳裡的情勢變複雜。我上回去廣東點心店，那裡有一個中文大告示：「請付小費。」

我想是因為大家覺得賓至如歸，所以忘了留小費。

Words & Phrases 詞彙片語

- tips (= To Insure Prompt Service) 小費（確保快速服務）
- magnificent 華麗的；高尚的；豐富的
- meal 餐；飯
- in years 多年來；長久來
- reciprocate 互換；酬答
- not a big deal 沒什麼了不起
- at least 至少
- three times as much 三倍於此
- excuse 原諒
- numbers 數字
- figure out 算出；想出
- civilized 文明的
- service charge 服務費
- customary 慣常的；合乎習俗的
- cab driver 計程車駕駛
- porter 機場、車站或旅館裡的行李搬運工
- meter （里程）表
- first-class 一流的
- instruct 指示；命令
- gratuities 小費；報酬
- revolution 革命

- introduce 引入（若和人連用則譯為「介紹」）
- on one's hand 成為自己的責任；手邊
- sort of 種類
- create 製造；創建
- complication 複雜；混亂
- notice 注意；通知
- Dim Sum（廣式）茶點
- sign 標誌；記號
- in Chinese 用中文
- request 要求
- feel at home 感覺自在；賓至如歸

A reminder 小提醒

在範文中用到了倍數「three times as much」，下面介紹倍數詞（half, double, treble/three times, four times, ...）的用法：

> The man bought a pre-owned car at half the original price.
> 這男人用半價買了一部二手車。
> I'll come back half an hour（= a half hour）later.
> 我在半小時後回來。
> He is double her age.
> 他是她年紀的兩倍。

但

> After the war, many things cost almost double.
>
> 戰後許多東西要花兩倍的錢。

此處的 double 是副詞，有別於先前例句中的形容詞 double。

Exercise 練習

利用括弧中所提供的字來改寫句子：

❶ That was the most magnificent meal I've had in years.

(splendid dinner, enjoyed, in many)

❷ A steak dinner would cost at least three times as much in Taipei.

(300 percent more, the least expensive)

❸ Now that's what I call a civilized system.

(institution, strikes me as, decent)

✽ splendid 壯觀的；豪華的；極好的

✽ percent 百分比

✽ least expensive 最便宜的

✽ institution 習俗；制度；機構

✽ strike me as 讓我覺得；給我印象

✽ decent 體面的；像樣的；正統的

Say It Differently 換種說法

Waiter Would you care for some dessert?

Eric How about you, Steve?

Steve Thanks, but I couldn't eat another bite. Maybe just a cup of coffee.

Eric OK, I guess we'll just have two coffees. Oh, and I'd like the check now, please.

Waiter Just a moment, sir.

* dessert 甜點
* check 帳單

Translation 譯文

Waiter 要不要來點甜點？

Eric 你呢，Steve？

Steve 謝了，但我一口都吃不下去了。也許來杯咖啡就好。

Eric 好的，我想我們只要兩杯咖啡。噢，請給我帳單。

Waiter 請等一下。

Answer Key 練習解答

❶ That was the most splendid dinner I've enjoyed in many years.

❷ The least expensive steak dinner would cost 300 percent more in Taipei.

❸ Now that strikes me as a decent institution.

The Way of Tipping

小費之道 (2)

Sample Conversation 範文

(The discussion on tipping continues.)

Steve At one Chinese restaurant I went to, the waiter brought me a bill that already included a 15 percent tip. Later I found out that they don't do that with their local customers, but with their Chinese clientele they're taking no chances.

Eric Is that a fact? Sometimes I get tired of the whole business, though. I rode a taxi once with a sign prominently displayed behind the driver's seat saying, "Gratuity not included in fare." Had to stare it the whole way to JFK. I don't care for that kind of pushy style.

Steve It's so cumbersome for us to figure out how much to tip. I saw a Japanese tourist who had given up. He was holding out a fistful of dollar bills to a taxi driver and letting him take what he wanted! But that's hardly an ideal solution either. Anyway, how did this all started, do you know?

Eric I understand it's an old English custom. There are a number of stories about the origin of the word "tip," but one I like best is that it's an acronym standing for "to insure promptness."

Steve Hmm, does that make sense? After all, you usually tip after you re-

ceive a service, not before, right?

 Actually, that's true, of course, and I admit the theory I gave you is probably nothing more than a folk etymology.

 Uh, I don't want to sound too inquisitive, but how much do you tip in a place like this?

 In a regular restaurant I'd give the waiter 15 percent of the total bill. Here I leave 20 percent.

Translation　譯文

（關於小費的對話持續中。）

 我去過一家中餐館，服務生給我已經加了 15% 小費的帳單。後來我發現他們並沒對當地客人做同樣的事，但他們對華裔客很小心。

 是嗎？但有時我對這整個事情感到厭煩。我曾有一次坐到一輛駕駛椅背有個顯著告示牌的計程車，上面說「小費不包含在車資內」。到甘迺迪機場前，我一路上都要盯著告示牌，我不喜歡那種一意孤行的做法。

 要算給多少小費真的很麻煩。我曾見過一位日本觀光客乾脆放棄，他手上握著一把美元鈔票讓計程車駕駛自己拿！但這也不是解決之道，你知道這是怎麼開始的嗎？

 我知道那是種古老的英國習俗，關於小費這個字的起源眾說紛紜，但我最喜歡的說法它是由英文的 to insure promtness 這組字字頭所組成。

 嗯，有理嗎？畢竟你通常在接受服務後而非之前給小費。

 那是當然，我承認我給你的說法可能也不過是民間流傳的字源說。

 我不想讓人聽起來愛打破砂鍋問到底，但像在這種地方你給多少小費？

Eric　在一般餐廳我會給服務生總價的 15%，在這裡我給 20%。

Words & Phrases 詞彙片語

- bill 帳單；鈔票
- local 本地的；鄉土的
- clientele 顧客；訴訟委託人
- take no chances 不冒險；謹慎行事的
- Is that a fact? 是嗎？
- get tired of 厭煩，厭倦
- the whole business 整件事
- prominently 顯著地；重要地
- display 顯示；陳列；炫耀
- stare 盯著看
- JFK（紐約）甘迺迪機場
- care for 喜歡
- pushy 堅持己見的；一意孤行的
- style 風格；時尚；式樣
- cumbersome 討厭的；麻煩的
- hold 拿著
- fistful 一把
- give up 放棄
- ideal 理想的
- hardly 幾乎不
- solution 解決之道

- stand for 代表
- acronym 首字母縮略字，由一連串字中每個字的第一個字母所組成能發音的縮寫字，例：

  Yuppie: Young Urban/Upward-mobile Professionals 雅痞，都會裡高收入的年輕專業人士

  DINK: Double Incomes, No Kids 頂客，雙薪收入但沒小孩的夫婦

  NIMBY: Never In My Back Yard 強烈反對在自己家附近建立如監獄或垃圾焚化爐等嫌惡設施的人

- promptness 快速
- make sense 講得通；有意義
- theory 理論；原理
- folk （流傳）民間的

  folk song 民歌，folklore 民間故事

- etymology 語源學
- inquisitive 好奇的；好問的
- regular 一般的；固定的；有規律的

A reminder 小提醒

有時，一個很簡單的片語，如 make no sense 也可以變成萬用無窮。

The answer made little sense to me.

這答案對我而言意義不大。

Your comments made a lot sense to the success of the proposal.

你的評論對成就整個企劃案的意義重大。

英文的使用在於是否能觸類旁通，字彙片語有限，但學會將其中關鍵字位置填入
其他的替代字，你會發現使用英文並不是那麼地難！

Exercise 練習

利用括弧中所提供的字來改寫句子：

❶ I don't care for that kind of pushy style.

(aggressive, object to)

❷ It's so cumbersome for us to figure out how much to tip.

(calculate, give the waiter, troublesome)

❸ That's hardly an ideal solution.

(not a good answer, to my dilemma)

✱ aggressive 積極行動的；侵略的；咄咄逼人的

✱ object to 反對

✱ calculate 計算；估計

✱ troublesome 麻煩的；棘手的

✱ dilemma 困境；進退兩難的局面

Say It Differently 換種說法

 Eric　(Put on glasses) Excuse me, I've now reached the age where I can't
read without these things.

 Steve　Do you always check the bill before you pay?

 Eric　It's a good idea. Sometimes they've added it up wrong, and a couple of times I've been given the bill for another party.

Steve　But at a fancy place like this...

Eric　Makes no difference. You still have to be careful.

Translation 譯文

Eric　（戴上眼鏡）對不起，我已經到了不戴眼鏡就什麼都看不到的年紀。

Steve　你總是會先檢查帳單再付錢嗎？

Eric　這是個好主意，有時他們算錯，有幾回我付了另外一群人的帳單。

Steve　但在如此華麗的地方 …

Eric　沒差，你還是得小心。

 put on　戴上

 glasses（老花）眼鏡

 reach　到達

 check　檢查

 add up　加起來

✱ party　當事人；聚會；黨派

✱ fancy　高價的；昂貴的；奇特的

✱ make no difference　沒影響的；沒關係的

Answer Key 練習解答

❶ I object to the kind of aggressive style.

❷ It's so troublesome for us to calculate how much to give the waiter.

❸ That's not a good answer to my dilemma.

The Way of Tipping

小費之道 (3)

 Sample Conversation 範文

(When in Rome, do as the Romans do.)

 Eric > Today I'm also giving $5 to the sommelier that is the wine steward, for his suggestion of a wine, which I thought was excellent. Oh, and it's customary to tip the coatroom attendant a dollar per coat and to give the doorman a dollar if he catches you a taxi.

 Steve > What if the service wasn't good? Can you leave without tipping?

 Eric > You could try it, but I wouldn't advise going back to that restaurant again. The way I see it, you should always leave something, because the tips are often an essential part of the employees' wages. If the service is lousy or nonexistent, you can always choose to go somewhere else next time. Also, on occasion I've written a polite letter to the management suggesting that the food or the service wasn't up to par.

 Steve > That seems like a lot of trouble to go to.

 Eric > If you can't be bothered to write a letter, I understand there's an organization that gives out preprinted complaint cards to its members. You can check off the items corresponding to your grievance and leave the card either in lieu of a tip or to explain why you left so little. In this particular restaurant, however, you really can't get out of the door without tipping. It's called the Palms, you see.

 Steve 〉 I don't get it.

 Eric 〉 Wait, I'll explain it to you once we're outside.

Translation 譯文

（入境隨俗。）

 Eric 〉 今天我也給酒侍五塊錢，因為我認為他推薦的酒好極了！噢，給衣帽間服務員一件外套一塊錢小費也是習俗，如果門房幫你叫計程車，也要給他一塊錢。

 Steve 〉 如果服務不好呢？你可不給小費就離開嗎？

 Eric 〉 你可以試試，但我不建議你下回再到那間餐廳。我的看法是你總該留點錢，因為小費是員工薪資中不可或缺的一部分。如果服務很糟或根本沒有，下回你總是能選擇去別的地方，而且有時我會給經理寫封禮貌的信，婉轉告訴他食物或服務不合標準。

 Steve 〉 好像很麻煩。

 Eric 〉 如果你不願意寫信，我知道有個提供會員事先印好的客訴卡的組織，你可以在不滿的項目裡打勾，以卡取代小費，或說明不給小費的原因，但在這家特別的餐廳，你很難不付小費就出門，你知道它的名字是「手掌」嗎？

 Steve 〉 我不懂。

Eric 〉 等下出去我再解釋。

Words & Phrases 詞彙片語

- sommelier 負責酒類的侍者
- steward 服務員
- coatroom（寄放）衣帽間
- attendant 服務員
- doorman 門房
- catch 搭上趕到計程車
- advise 建議（動詞）
- the way I see it 我的看法是 …
- essential 不可或缺的
- wage 時薪
- lousy 差勁的；汙穢的；噁心的
- nonexistent 不存在的
- up to par 合乎標準

  par 高爾夫球中的標準桿
- preprinted 事先印好的
- complaint 抱怨；抗議；控訴
- check off 核對；清點
- item 項目；商品
- corresponding 對應的；一致的
- grievance 不滿；苦衷；牢騷
- in lieu of 代替
- palms 棕櫚樹；手掌（不給小費小心打你！）

💬　I don't get it. 我不明白。

▌ A reminder 小提醒

essential 和 necessary 雖然意思相同，但在使用上會有不同含意。

> Most authorities agree that play is an essential part in children's development.
>
> 大部分權威人士同意遊玩在孩童發展上是必要的。
>
> Capital is necessary in setting up one's own business.
>
> 資金是成立個人事業中必須的。

遊戲在孩童發展中是一個不可或缺的活動，但資金則未必是事業成功必要的條件。

✎ Exercise 練習

利用括弧中所提供的字來改寫句子：

① What if the service wasn't good?

　(How about if, was below par)

② The way I see it, you should always leave something.

　(in my opinion, all the time, you'd better)

③ You can always choose to go somewhere else next time.

　(the same place, not to, return)

✳　what if 如果

* below par 水準以下；不盡理想
* all the time 始終；總是；時時刻刻

Say It Differently 換種說法

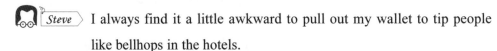

Steve I always find it a little awkward to pull out my wallet to tip people like bellhops in the hotels.

Eric My system there is to take the money out of my billfold in advance and have it ready in my pocket.

Steve But what if you don't have the right amount?

Eric That can be a problem. I try to keep a good supply of singles on hand, especially when I'm traveling.

Translation 譯文

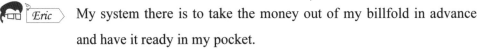

Steve 掏錢包付小費給飯店門房總會讓我覺得尷尬。

Eric 我的做法是事先把錢從皮夾裡拿出來放在口袋裡。

Steve 但萬一你沒有正確的數額呢？

Eric 那問題就大了，我會儘量在手邊保持足夠的一元紙鈔，尤其是在旅行的時候。

* awkward 尷尬的；難處理的；笨拙的
* wallet（男性）皮夾
* bellhop 侍者；旅館的行李員
* billfold 皮夾

✱ in advance 事先

✱ have...ready 將 … 準備妥當

✱ pocket 口袋

✱ amount 數額

✱ a good supply of 足夠的

✱ singles 一元紙幣

Answer Key 練習解答

❶ How about if the service was below par?

❷ In my opinion, you'd better leave something all the time.

❸ You can always choose not to return to the same place.

A Night out

交際應酬 (1)

Sample Conversation 範文

(Steve Lee is taking John Spencer, an oversea business associate, out for a treat.)

Steve ▷ I'd like to take you out tonight. Is there anything you'd especially like to see or do – or any restaurant you're particularly interested in having dinner at?

John ▷ Thank you, Steve. That's very thoughtful of you. When I was here three years ago, someone took me to a fancy restaurant. I was grateful for his kindness, but that wasn't my cup of tea. Let's go to some quaint little restaurant where not many foreign tourists go.

Steve ▷ Do you care for Chinese food?

John ▷ Oh, I love it.

Steve ▷ You have no problem with some exotic dishes?

John ▷ No problem at all. I'm an adventurous eater.

Steve ▷ All right, I'll take you to a nice Chinese restaurant that features country-style cuisine. Is that all right?

John ▷ Sure. That sounds very intriguing.

Steve ▷ What time shall we go?

John ▷ Whenever. Shall we say 6 or 6:30?

Steve ▷ OK, I'll meet you in the main lobby of the hotel at 6:30.

John Super. See you then.

Translation 譯文

（Steve Lee 請海外同事 John Spencer 出去吃飯。）

Steve 我想今晚帶你出去，有沒有你特別想看或想做的事，或到任何你特別
想去的餐廳吃晚餐？

John Steve，謝謝你。你真是周到，當我三年前來此地時，有人帶我去一間
豪華餐廳，我對他的熱情很感激，但那並非我所喜歡的。我們去外國
觀光客很少去的典雅餐廳吧。

Steve 你想吃中國食物嗎？

John 噢，我愛死了！

Steve 你對異國食物沒問題？

John 一點問題都沒有，我是個愛嘗鮮的吃客。

Steve 好，我帶你去個以鄉土菜為特色的中餐廳，可以嗎？

John 好啊，聽起來很有趣。

Steve 我們幾點去？

John 任何時間，6 點或 6 點半如何？

Steve 好，我 6 點半會在旅館大廳和你見面。

John 棒透了，到時候見。

Words & Phrases 詞彙片語

● oversea 國外的；海外的

- associate 同事;合夥人

- treat 款待;樂事

- especially 特別地;格外地

- thoughtful 體貼的;周到的;深思熟慮的

- grateful 感激的

- kindness 仁慈;善行;友好的行為

- cup of tea 和某人胃口;受某人喜愛的

- quaint 古雅的;奇特有趣的

- care for 喜歡;計較;尊重

- exotic 異國情調的;奇特的

- dish 菜

- adventurous 喜歡冒險的;大膽的

- feature 以…為特色/號召

- country-style 鄉村的

- cuisine 菜肴;料理

- intriguing 有趣的;迷人的;引起好奇的

- lobby 大廳

- super 超級的;頂呱呱的

▌◀ A reminder 小提醒

「super」在本段範文中出現,除了我們習以為常的意思外,它變成了一種非常口語化的表現。在英文中,口語、俚語的例證不勝枚舉:

airhead: 愚蠢的人　　　ball: 好玩的時光　　　chicken: 懦夫

dicey: 危險的；難以預測的　　eyeball: 長時間盯著人看

far out: 棒透了　　　get it: 了解；明白　　　hairy: 危險；困難

icky: 討厭的　　　jerk: 討厭的人　　　knockout: 美女

laid back: 放輕鬆　　　mickey-mouse: 不重要的；浪費時間的

neat: 很棒　　　off your face: 爛醉　　　peanuts: 非常少的錢

rip off: 偷　　　shades: 太陽眼鏡　　　up for it: 願意去做 …

veg out: 看電視；打發時間；休閒；逍遙　　　wad: 很多錢

X-rated: 色情的　　　Yank: 美國人　　　zip up: 閉嘴

Exercise 練習

利用括弧裡所提供的字來改寫句子：

❶ I'd like to take you out tonight.

(have dinner, I wish to, with)

❷ I was grateful for his kindness, but that wasn't my cup of tea.

(appreciated, thoughtfulness, like the place)

❸ You have no problem with some exotic dishes?

(is there, any)

✽ appreciate 感激、感謝；欣賞、賞識

☀ Say It Differently 換種說法

> Steve 〉 May I take you out for dinner tonight, if you're free?

> John 〉 Thank you. That's very kind of you.

> Steve 〉 Do you have a preference as to the kind of restaurant we go to?

> John 〉 I like Chinese food but I'll leave it up to you. I do have one slight problem though. I am allergic to eggs.

> Steve 〉 All right. Do you like sea food and stuff like that?

> John 〉 Yes. I often have seafood platter for appetizer.

◔ Translation 譯文

> Steve 〉 如果你有空，我今晚能請你去吃晚飯嗎？

> John 〉 謝謝你的好意。

> Steve 〉 你對去哪種餐廳有特別的偏愛嗎？

> John 〉 我喜歡中餐，但還是由你選，只是我有一個小毛病，我對蛋過敏。

> Steve 〉 好的，你喜歡海鮮類嗎？

> John 〉 是的，我常以海鮮拼盤當開胃菜。

❋ preference 喜愛；偏愛

❋ leave...to someone 交由⋯決定

❋ slight 細小的

❋ allergic to 對⋯過敏

❋ stuff 素材；資料；東西

❋ seafood platter 海鮮拼盤

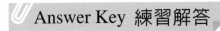

Answer Key 練習解答

❶ I wish to have dinner with you tonight.

❷ I appreciated his thoughtfulness, but I didn't like the place.

❸ Is there any problem with some exotic dishes?

A Night out

交際應酬 (2)

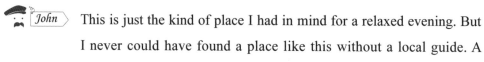

⟨ Sample Conversation 範文

(The night of eating continues.)

John This is just the kind of place I had in mind for a relaxed evening. But I never could have found a place like this without a local guide. A good choice, Steve.

Steve I'm glad you like it, John.

John Now what are these?

Steve This is Fried Sea Cucumber with Spring Onion, this is Fish with Assorted Vegetable Broth, and this is Braised Abalone in Brown Sauce. They are my favorites. You did say you were adventurous, didn't you?

John Perhaps not that adventurous. Hmm, this is not bad. Tell me, how was your trip to the US last time?

Steve I thought it was very worthwhile for me to see the operations over there and get to know my counterparts.

John Oh, yes, it's very important to know the key people on the other end. Now, is this rice wine?

Steve Yes. It's been warmed. Do you prefer it cold?

John No, I like it just the way it is. By the way, perhaps you could help me with a question I had. Some of my associates were talking about hav-

ing to accept promissory notes. I didn't quite understand what was
going on.

Translation 譯文

（應酬進行中。）

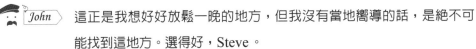

John 這正是我想好好放鬆一晚的地方，但我沒有當地嚮導的話，是絕不可能找到這地方。選得好，Steve。

Steve 我很高興你喜歡，John。

John 哇，這些是什麼？

Steve 這是蔥燒海參，這是蔬菜魚湯，這是紅燒鮑魚。它們是我的最愛，你說過你喜歡嘗鮮，對吧？

John 也許沒那麼愛冒險。嗯，味道不錯。告訴我你上回的美國之旅如何？

Steve 我覺得看到那裡的運作以及認識一些同等級的夥伴相當值得。

John 對的，知道另一頭的關鍵人物是很重要的。這是米酒嗎？

Steve 是的，溫過的。你比較喜歡冷的嗎？

John 不，這樣剛好。對了，也許你能給我答案。我的一些同事在討論接受本票的事，而我不太了解這回事。

Words & Phrases 詞彙片語

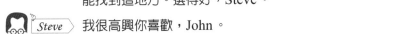

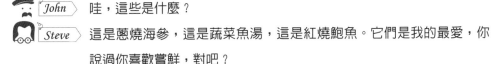

- to have in mind 想到；打算
- relaxed 輕鬆自在的；無拘無束的
- guide 嚮導

- sea cucumber 海參
- spring onion 蔥
- fried sea cucumber with spring onion 蔥燒海參
- assorted 綜合的；什錦的
- broth （用菜或肉煮成的）清湯
- fish with assorted vegetable broth 蔬菜魚湯
- braised 燉熟的；爛熟的
- abalone 鮑魚
- sauce 調味汁；醬汁
- braised abalone in brown sauce 紅燒鮑魚
- worthwhile 值得的
- counterpart 對等的人物
- key 主要的；關鍵的
- rice wine 米酒；紹興酒
- promissory note 本票；期票

▌A reminder 小提醒

中餐料理手法形形色色：

grill: 烤；燒	bake: 烘	casserole: 砂鍋	boil: 水煮	braise: 紅燒
broil: 高溫烤	fry: 炒	simmer fry: 扒	pan-fry: 煎	roast: 燒臘
sauté: 煸	simmer: 燉；煨		smoke: 燻	steam: 蒸
stew: 煲	stir-fry: 翻炒			

就連準備食材的方法也都是琳瑯滿目：

beat: 搗成糊狀	break: 打斷；打破	chop: 剁	crush: 壓碎
cut: 切	dice: 切丁	end: 去根	grate: 刨絲
grind: 磨	julienne: 切絲	peel: 削皮	scrub: 刷
shell: 剝殼	shred: 切條	slice: 切薄片	soak: 浸泡
split: 切開	squeeze: 擠	stir: 攪拌	trim: 修剪

請外國朋友吃中國菜，不僅是要好吃，更要能將中餐準備和烹飪時的步驟、做法做說明，如此才能賓主盡歡！

Exercise 練習

利用括弧裡所提供的字來改寫句子：

❶ I never could have found a place like this without a local guide.

(you need a native, a restaurant, hit)

❷ Tell me, how was your trip to the US last time?

(how, went, I wonder)

❸ It's very important to know the key people on the other end.

(knowing, a necessity, is)

✳ native　本地人

✳ hit　碰上

✳ necessity　必需（品）

☀ Say It Differently 換種說法

John > Do you see a lot of night life?

Steve > I'm not really the "night on the town" type. I very seldom go barhopping, if that's what you mean.

John > There seem to be millions of drinking establishments in major night spots in Taipei. Do they mostly cater to customers doing business entertaining?

Steve > Not necessarily, though business entertainment is big business in Taiwan, now golf is used quite frequently to entertain customers too.

◖ Translation 譯文

John > 你常過夜生活嗎？

Steve > 我不是那種都會夜貓子，我很少續攤，如果這是你想講的。

John > 在臺北主要夜生活地區好像有很多喝酒的地方，他們通常是做商務應酬的嗎？

Steve > 儘管商務應酬這塊在臺灣很賺，但也不盡然。現在打高爾夫球來應酬客戶也很頻繁。

✳ night life 夜生活

✳ night on the town 在城市裡尋歡作樂

✳ seldom 很少；難得；不常

✳ barhopping 從這家酒店喝到那家酒店

✳ establishment 建立的機關、公司、企業

✴ night spot　夜總會；夜店

✴ cater to　為 … 服務；迎合

Answer Key 練習解答

❶ You need a native to hit a restaurant like this.

❷ I wonder how your trip to the US went last time.

❸ Knowing the key people on the other end is a necessity.

A Night out

交際應酬 (3)

Sample Conversation 範文

(It's more than a meal.)

 John   What's a promissory note?

 Steve   It's a written promise to pay a designated amount at a certain future time – usually three to six months.

 John   Six months! At no interest?

 Steve   No interest. Some notes aren't payable for 9 to 12 months.

 John   We can't afford to work like that. It will have a terrible effect on our cash flow.

 Steve   Taiwanese companies sometimes pay their suppliers in promissory notes. Once a hotel chain offered to pay us half in promissory notes and half in accommodation coupons. We declined.

 John   Don't they realize that you're not a bank? What are we getting now?

 Steve   This is what we call squid noodles. And these are monkfish liver and sea urchin. They may not sound very good, but actually they're real delicacies.

 John   Do you often go out drinking with your colleagues after work?

 Steve   Yes. I'm a great believer in nomunication.

 John   What's that supposed to mean?

 Steve It's a combination of the Japanese word nomu, which means to drink, and communication. It means you can communicate better through drinking.

Translation 譯文

（不只是吃飯。）

John 本票是什麼？

Steve 是一種在未來某個時間點，通常是三到六個月，支付指定金額的書面契約。

John 六個月！沒有利息？

Steve 沒利息，一些本票九到十二個月才支付。

John 我們不能承受這種狀況，對我們的資金周轉有很嚴重的影響。

Steve 臺灣公司有時用本票支付給供應商。有一次一家連鎖旅館要一半用本票一半用住宿折價券來支付我們公司，我們拒絕了。

John 難道他們不知道你們不是銀行嗎？我們現在吃的是什麼？

Steve 這是我們所謂的花枝麵，這是鮟鱇魚肝和海膽，聽起來可能不好聽，但它們是真的美食。

John 你常在下班後和同事一起去喝酒嗎？

Steve 是的，我是「拚酒搏感情」的信仰者。

John 那是什麼意思？

Steve 它是日文 nomu 喝酒和 communication 兩個字的合體。它的意思是藉著喝酒，交情會更好。

Words & Phrases 詞彙片語

written promise 書面承諾

designated 指定的

amount 數量;總額

interest 利息

payable 可付的;應付的

afford 負擔得起

terrible 可怕的;極壞的

effect 效果;影響

cash flow 現金流量

supplier 供應商

offer 提供;出價

accommodation 住宿

coupon 優惠券

squid noodle 花枝麵

monkfish 鮟鱇魚

liver 肝(臟)

sea urchin 海膽

combination 組合

communicate 溝通;表達

A reminder 小提醒

「can't afford to」是個常見的表達，不僅和 can 連用，afford 也常和 be able to 連用，主要用於否定句和疑問句：

> Time is the luxury we can't afford in getting the job done.
>
> 要把事情做好，時間是個大問題。
>
> Labor-heavy is a factor that none of us is able to afford to neglect.
>
> 對人力的依賴是我們所有人都無法忽視的因素。

雖然中文多譯成「供得起」，但實際上多具有否定的含意。

另外，「sometime」「sometimes」和「some time」的意思也大不相同：

> I sometimes go to work on foot.
>
> 我有時步行上班。
>
> I will see you sometime in the future.
>
> 我將在將來某個時間和你見面。
>
> I will need some time to think about your proposal.
>
> 我需要一些時間來考慮你的建議。

Exercise 練習

利用括弧中所提供的字來改寫句子：

❶ It'll have a terrible effect on our cash flow.

(adversely affect)

❷ Taiwanese companies sometimes pay their suppliers in promissory notes.

(use, in paying, corporations)

❸ Don't they realize that you're not a bank?

(provide, banking service, understand)

✱ adversely 不利地；敵對地

✱ affect 影響；妨礙

✱ corporation 公司；法人；社團

✱ provide 提供

✱ banking service 金融服務

☼ Say It Differently 換種說法

 Steve There's a notion in Taiwan that unless you drink together, you can't form close human ties.

 John Here's to our close human ties, Steve.

 Steve Cheers.

 John Drinking places seem to be crowded with businessmen after office hours.

 Steve Yes, it's a good way for them to unwind. Alcohol also loosens the tongue and lets people speak their minds. You can get their honest sentiments, which are otherwise often covered behind the poker face.

Translation 譯文

Steve　在臺灣有個觀念，除非你們一起喝酒，否則人脈無法拉近。

John　這杯敬我們之間的關係。

Steve　敬你。

John　喝酒的地方似乎在下班後都擠滿生意人。

Steve　是的，這是讓他們放鬆的好方法。酒精能讓人鬆口暢所欲言，你能得到那些常隱藏在撲克臉後的實話。

* notion　觀念；想法
* form　形成
* close　緊密的
* human ties　人際關係
* cheer　為 … 喝采
* crowded　擁擠的
* unwind　放鬆；解開
* alcohol　酒精
* loosen　鬆開
* tongue　舌頭
  to loosen one's tongue　大放厥詞
* to speak one's mind　直言不諱
* honest　誠實的；真摯的
* sentiment　感情；意見
* otherwise　否則

✱ cover 覆蓋；掩飾

✱ poker face 撲克臉；沒有表情的

Answer Key 練習解答

❶ It'll adversely affect our cash flow.

❷ Taiwanese corporations sometimes use promissory notes in paying their suppliers.

❸ Don't they understand that you don't provide banking service?

By the Book

照章行事

Sample Conversation 範文

(Steve Lee found himself in the hot seat.)

Nancy Oh, Steve, Henry Sherman of Financial Operations just called. He said it was urgent. Do you suppose there's some problem?

Steve Well, those bean counters always want something done yesterday. They also tend to have an inflated view of their own importance, I've found, as if the future of the company rested entirely in their hands. Wait a minute. Maybe he wants to talk to me about the expense report I submitted the other day.

Steve Were you looking for me, Henry?

Henry Oh, Steve. Please come in. How are you today?

Steve Keeping alive. And you?

Henry Fine, thanks. Sorry to take your time now. I know you're quite busy on that strategic alliance project.

Steve It's all right. What can I do for you, chief?

Henry Well, it's about the statement you submitted for your trip to the States. I think there may be some slight misunderstandings on your part about corporate policy on travel expenses. It's no big problem and I'm

sure we can clear it right up if you'll allow me to ask a few questions. All right?

Steve > Fair enough.

Henry > Very well. You indicated on your expense sheet that you stayed at a hotel for five nights and that it cost you $100 a night. But you attach no receipt. Now I know how expensive decent hotels are in the States and for safety considerations I would not advise any of our employees to stay in a 100-dollar-a-night place.

Translation 譯文

（Steve Lee 發現自己處境尷尬。）

Nancy > 噢！Steve，財務部的 Henry Sherman 剛打電話來。他說是急事，你認為哪裡有問題嗎？

Steve > 那些會計總想昨天就把事情做好，我發現他們也有自我膨風的傾向，就好像公司的未來在他們手中一樣。等一下，也許他想和我談談我那天交的費用報告。

Steve > Henry，你找我嗎？

Henry > Steve，請進來。你今天如何？

Steve > 還好啦，你呢？

Henry > 很好，謝謝。我知道你在忙那個策略合作計畫，但很抱歉，現在要占用你的時間。

Steve > 沒關係。我能為你做什麼嗎，老大？

Henry > 是關於你交的美國之行的開支報表，我想你可能對公司旅行經費政策

上有些小誤解，但這問題不大。如果你容許我問你幾個問題，我很確定我們可以馬上弄清楚，好嗎？

Steve 好吧。

Henry 很好，你在你開支報表上指出你在旅館待了五晚，一晚的費用是 100 美元，但你沒有附收據。我知道在美國像樣的旅館費用有多高，為了安全起見，我不建議員工住在一晚 100 美元的旅館。

Words & Phrases 詞彙片語

- in the hot seat 擔負重任；處境尷尬艱難
- financial 財務的
- operation 作業；運作
- suppose 猜想；推測；認為
- bean counter 會計人員（多有輕蔑之意；計算小錢的人）
- inflated 誇張的；膨風的
- view 觀點；看法
- as if 好像
- rest 依賴；繫於
- entirely 完全地
- expense report 支出開銷報告
- submit 提交；呈送
- alive 活著的；有生氣的；活潑的
- strategic alliance 策略性聯盟
- chief 首領（開玩笑的用法）
- statement 書面報告

- slight 些微的

- on one's part 在 … 部分

- corporate policy 公司政策

- clear up 澄清；釐清

- fair enough 好吧，我接受

- indicate 指出

- expense sheet 開銷表

- attach 附上

- receipt 收據

- decent 像樣的

- safety consideration 安全考量

- advise 建議

◀ A reminder 小提醒

「as if」是一種假設語氣的用法，除了一般使用「wish」來表示外，還有下列的
句型也代表了假設語氣：

It seems as though it might rain.

看來好像要下雨。

But for you, I would have been drowned.

= If it had not been for you, I would have been drowned.

若非你，我就淹死了。

With your advice, I should certainly succeed.

有了你的建議，我一定會成功。

The situation could be saved by immediate action.

The situation could be saved if we took immediate action.

這狀況可經由立即的行動來解救。

She was ill that day; otherwise, she would have taken part in the meeting.

她那天生病,否則她就會出席會議。

Exercise 練習

利用括弧裡所提供的字來改寫句子:

❶ Those bean counters always want something done yesterday.

(accountants, in a hurry, to get something done)

❷ It's about the statement you submitted for your trip to the States.

(turned in, I want to talk to you, the States visit)

❸ There may be slight misunderstandings on your part.

(perhaps, a few things, you misunderstand)

✱ accountants 會計

✱ in a hurry 匆忙地

✱ to get something done 把事做好

✱ turn in 交繳

Say It Differently 換種說法

 Steve The last thing I need today is to get stuck in a session with our esteemed accountant. I have to visit two customers this afternoon and the headquarters is on my back for my quarterly sales projections. Could you ask Henry if it can wait?

Nancy Certainly, but don't you think it might be more effective if you call him yourself? He may prefer telling you what it's about personally.

 Steve OK. I'll give him a call and see if I can get a reprieve.

Translation 譯文

 Steve 我今天最不需要的就是和我們可敬的會計混一天,我下午必須去拜訪兩位客戶,而總部又一直追著我要季銷售預估報表,你可以問 Henry 這件事能不能等?

Nancy 沒問題,但你不覺得如果你自己打電話給他會更有效?他也許比較想親自告訴你和何事有關。

 Steve 好的,我打個電話給他看是否能暫緩。

 ✱ get stuck in 陷在

✱ esteemed 受人尊敬的

 ✱ headquarters 總部

✱ session 一場;一段時間

✱ on one's back 難以擺脫的 …

✱ quarterly(每)季的

✱ sales projections 銷售預測

✱ effective 有效果

✱ what it's about 和⋯有關

✱ personally 親自

✱ reprieve 暫緩；暫免

Answer Key 練習解答

① Those accountants are always in a hurry to get something done.

② I want to talk to you about the statement you turned in for the States visit.

③ Perhaps you misunderstand a few things.

Ins and Outs of Expense Report

費用報告細節

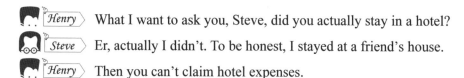

Sample Conversation 範文

(Steve Lee got a lesson of ins and outs about expenses.)

Henry > What I want to ask you, Steve, did you actually stay in a hotel?

Steve > Er, actually I didn't. To be honest, I stayed at a friend's house.

Henry > Then you can't claim hotel expenses.

Steve > But I bought a gift to bring to my host and I also took him and his wife out for a night on the town to thank them for putting me up. So I thought I'd bill the company half of what a hotel would've cost me so as to cover my expenses.

Henry > I'm sorry, Steve, but you may not exercise that kind of arbitrary judgment. If you spent money in lieu of hotel expenses, you should charge it under "other expenses" with itemization of the gift and entertainment. Did you keep the receipts?

Steve > I guess so.

Henry > Good. Now, I see you're requesting a per diem of $50 for six days.

Steve > Isn't that the standard amount to cover the cost of meals?

Henry > Yes, it is. But I presume that you had breakfast and perhaps some other meals at your friend's place. And I imagine your contact people in the States took you out for lunch or dinner, at least once, am I wrong?

 Steve No, but...

Henry Technically the cost of those meals should be deducted from the per diem. In your case, it's probably better to enter the actual out-of-pocket expenses that you personally paid for, along with verification.

Translation 譯文

（Steve Lee 學到了關於費用細節的經驗。）

Henry Steve，我想問你的是你有沒有住在旅館？

Steve 嗯，實際上我沒有。老實說，我住在一位朋友家裡。

Henry 那麼你不能申請住宿費用。

Steve 但我為房屋主人買了份禮物而且有天晚上我帶他和他太太進城，謝謝他們收留我，所以我想我可以把住旅館會花費的一半開銷，支付我的花費。

Henry 我很抱歉，Steve，但你不可以使用那種隨心所欲的判斷，如果你用其他花費來替代，你該把它列舉在以禮物和娛樂為名的「其他開銷」。

Steve 我想是吧！

Henry 好，現在我看到你要求六天每天 50 美元的出差津貼。

Steve 那不是用來支付餐費的標準額度嗎？

Henry 是的，但我想你有在你朋友家吃早餐也許還有午晚餐。我猜你在美國的聯絡人也會至少一次帶你出去吃午或晚餐，我錯了嗎？

Steve 沒有，但 …

Henry 嚴格地說，那些餐點的費用該從每天的津貼中扣除。在你的狀況中，你最好用自己掏腰包的方式，連同證明來辦理。

Words & Phrases 詞彙片語

- ins and outs 裡裡外外；詳細情形
- to be honest 說實話
- claim 要求；索賠
- host 主人
- put up 提供食宿；忍受；公布；張貼
- bill (v.) 送帳單給 …
- cover (v.) 足夠支付
- exercise (v.) 行使；適用
- arbitrary 隨心所欲的；武斷的
- judgment 判斷
- in lieu of 替代
- charge (v.) 索價；記載帳上
- itemization 按項列出
- per diem 按日計算的津貼；出差津貼
- imagine 想像
- contact (n.) 聯絡人
- technically 嚴格地說；技術上地
- deduct 扣除；減除
- in your case 在你的個案中
- actual 實際的；真正的
- out-of-pocket 自掏腰包
- verification 證明；確認；核實

A reminder 小提醒

「per diem」是個拉丁語，相當於「per day」，諺語中有「carpe diem」「seize the day」（把握今天）的用法。

另外，和 per 常連用的字詞有：

per annum（每一年）、per capita（每一個人）、percent（百分比）、perse（本質）

在公司上班，出差是難免。下列的字或許能有所幫助：

lodging/accommodation allowance　住宿費

daily allowance　每日零用金

meal allowance（誤）餐費

Exercise 練習

利用括弧裡所提供的字來改寫句子：

❶ To be honest, I stayed at a friend's house in the States.

(my friend, honestly speaking, put me up)

❷ Then you can't claim hotel expenses.

(charge the company, in that case, accommodations)

❸ I presume that you had breakfast and some other meals at your friend's place.

(house, ate, take it)

* in that case 既然那樣
* accommodation 住宿
* take it 假設；認為

☀ Say It Differently 換種說法

Henry　Tell me, Steve, what was the name of this budget-priced hotel?

Steve　Er, it was called the...

Henry　Let's stop playing games with each other. You didn't stay in any hotel, did you?

Steve　(Hesitates) No.

Henry　Steve, I hope you realize that a falsified expense report is no laughing matter.

Steve　I know, but can I explain?

◖ Translation 譯文

Henry　告訴我，Steve，那家廉價旅館的名字是什麼？

Steve　呃，它叫 …

Henry　我們兩個都別再演了，你沒住在旅館，有嗎？

Steve　（猶豫）沒有。

Henry　Steve，我希望你了解開支報表造假不是鬧著玩的。

Steve　我知道，但我能解釋嗎？

* budget-priced 價格低廉的

✱ play games with 耍心機

✱ falsified 造假的

✱ no laughing matter 不是鬧著玩的

Answer Key 練習解答

❶ Honestly speaking, my friend in the States put me up.

❷ In that case, you can't charge the company for accommodation.

❸ I take it that you ate breakfast and some other meals at your friend's house.

The Lecture Continues

繼續說教

◯ Sample Conversation 範文

(Steve Lee felt like a child!)

 Henry   If it was a business meal, put it down under "entertainment," and be sure to include the name of the other party and your business relationship with them. Incidentally, company policy is that the per diem and actual costs may not be mixed during the same trip. You have to opt for one or the other.

 Steve   Oh, I didn't know that. Anyway, I'm sorry. I'll be more careful with my expense reports in the future.

 Henry   No need to apologize. I'm sure there'll be no further problems once you understand the proper procedures. I think I'll send out a general memorandum just to be sure everybody understands our expense account policy. Oh, one more thing. Steve. You've put down several "miscellaneous." What are they?

 Steve   Let's see, that refers to money for the porters at the airport, a shoe-shine, a haircut and some newspapers.

 Henry   In that case, you can charge for porterage but no other expenses, since they're of a personal nature. As a matter of principle, an expense report should not include the term miscellaneous. Specify the actual

item.

Steve > Yes, sir.

Henry > Sorry, Steve. I didn't mean to be too hard on you. Please don't take it personally. And I want to commend you on promptness of your report.

Steve > Thank you. Will that be all?

Translation 譯文

（Steve Lee 覺得自己像個（做錯事的）孩子。）

Henry > 如果是公事餐點，把它記在「娛樂」項目，但要確定把對方名字和彼此業務關係寫進去。對了，公司規定同一趟出差的差旅津貼和實際花費不能混在一起，你一定要在兩個中選一個。

Steve > 那我不知道。總之，我很抱歉。以後我寫開支報表會更小心。

Henry > 不需要道歉，一旦你了解正確流程後，我確定你不會有別的問題的。我想有必要發給大家公司章程，確定大家都了解公司的會計政策。還有一件事，Steve。你有幾項「雜支」，它們是什麼啊？

Steve > 讓我看看，那是支付機場行李搬運工、擦鞋、理髮和報紙的錢。

Henry > 如果是那樣，你可以申請搬運費但其他費用不行，因為這些均屬私人消費。原則上，雜項這名稱不該被包含在開支報表中。你要具體說明實際項目。

Steve > 是的，長官。

Henry > 很抱歉，Steve。我不想對你太刁難，千萬別認為是人身攻擊。而且我要嘉獎你迅速交報表一事。

Steve > 謝謝你，還有別的事嗎？

Words & Phrases 詞彙片語

- lecture 說教
- be sure 確定
- party 當事人
- incidentally 順便一提
- mix 混雜
- opt for 選擇
- in the future 未來
- apologize 道歉
- procedure 程序；手續
- general 一般性的
- memorandum (memo) 備忘錄
- miscellaneous 雜項
- porter 腳伕；搬運行李的人
- shoeshine 擦鞋攤
- porterage 運輸的
- nature 性質；本質
- a matter of principle 原則問題
- specify 具體說明；詳細指名
- be hard on 刁難
- personally 人身攻擊地
- commend 嘉獎
- promptness 迅速的；準時的

💬 Will that be all? 還有其他的事嗎？

🔊 A reminder 小提醒

「memorandum」也是個拉丁字，簡寫成「memo」，複數形可寫成「memoran-dums」或「memoranda」。

名詞的複數形變化是英文中常出現問題的地方，到底是規則地在字尾加「s」、「es」還是「ies」，或是不規則地變化？

> datum – data 資訊、referendum – referenda 公民投票
>
> analysis – analyses 分析、thesis – thesis 論文
>
> phenomenon – phenomena 現象

單複數的變化不可不小心！

Exercise 練習

利用括弧裡所提供的字來寫句子：

❶ Be sure to include the name of the other party.

  (mention, who you had the business lunch with, don't forget)

❷ No need to apologize.

  (don't, have to)

❸ I want to commend you on the promptness of your report.

  (promptly, you should be congratulated, turning in)

✱ mention 提及；說道

✱ promptly 迅速地

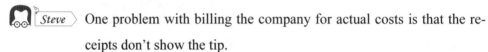

Say It Differently 換種說法

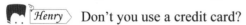

Steve One problem with billing the company for actual costs is that the receipts don't show the tip.

Henry Don't you use a credit card?

Steve Often I do, but what difference does that make?

Henry Instead of tipping in cash, write in the tip on the credit card slip and submit it with your receipt. Oh, and don't forget to write the total charge on the line provided.

Translation 譯文

Steve 向公司報實際開銷的問題是收據上並沒有顯示出小費。

Henry 你沒用信用卡嗎？

Steve 我常用，但有差別嗎？

Henry 把小費寫在信用卡簽單上，把簽單和收據一起繳交。別忘了把總數寫在裡面的直線上。

✱ credit card 信用卡

✱ What difference does it make? 有什麼區別呢？

✱ instead of 代替

✱ slip 紙條；簽帳條

Answer Key 練習解答

❶ Don't forget to mention who you had the business lunch with.

❷ You don't have to apologize.

❸ You should be congratulated for turning in your report promptly.

Even a Well-organized Person Can't Find It

神仙也幫不上忙

Sample Conversation 範文

(Someone is having a hard time finding the documents.)

Nancy　Steve, sorry to bother you about such a trifling matter as this but Mike Collins is looking for a copy of the feasibility report on telemarketing conducted by our management consultants. He says he can't find it in any of his files. Actually I'm not surprised. You know the way he stacks up piles of paper all over his office. This is the third time he's come to me for a missing document.

Steve　Don't be too upset, Nancy. Give him a copy of my report. I have it right here in my desk-size cabinet. Here you go.

Nancy　You are a well-organized person, aren't you? You always know which file to go to for any information. How do you manage to do that?

Steve　Well, not always. But I learned my system from Paul Jones. Remember he used to say, "If you don't know where a document is, it might as well not exist." I use broad generic headings, the way he did because overly specific labels are hard to remember. This report was filed under "Marketing."

Nancy　I see. But you also weed out documents from time to time as part of keeping your files updated, don't you? I wish everybody else did that.

Our file cabinets are bursting with paper.

Steve I have an idea. Maybe we need a "paper-chase day."

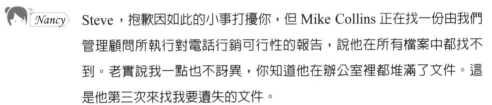
Translation 譯文

（有人找不到文件了。）

Nancy Steve，抱歉因如此的小事打擾你，但 Mike Collins 正在找一份由我們管理顧問所執行對電話行銷可行性的報告，說他在所有檔案中都找不到。老實說我一點也不訝異，你知道他在辦公室裡都堆滿了文件。這是他第三次來找我要遺失的文件。

Steve 別煩了，Nancy，把我的報告再印一份給他。我就放在我辦公桌上的檔案櫃內，給妳。

Nancy 你是個有組織的人，對吧？你總是知道去哪個檔案找資料，你是如何辦到的？

Steve 並不總是如此，但我從 Paul Jones 那裡學到這套系統，記得他曾說過如果你不知道一份文件在哪裡，你那份文件可能根本就不存在了。我如他一樣用廣義的總稱標題，因為太過專門的標題很難記住。這份報告是放在行銷名下。

Nancy 我知道了，但你也常剔除文件來使你的檔案更新，不是嗎？我希望所有人都能那樣做，我們的檔案櫃總是塞滿了文件。

Steve 我們需要個文件清理日。

Words & Phrases 詞彙片語

- document 文件;文檔;紀錄
- bother 打攪;煩擾
- trifling 不重要的;無聊的
- feasibility 可行性
- telemarketing 電話行銷
- management consultant 經營顧問
- file (n.) 文件夾;檔案;卷宗
- stack 堆放
- pile 堆;疊
- missing 失蹤的
- be upset 心煩意亂的;不舒服的
- desk-size 書桌大小;適合置於桌面上的
- cabinet 櫥櫃;內閣
- here you go 給你
- well-organized 工作有條理的;妥備完善的
- manage to 設法;成功完成
- used to (過去的)習慣
- might as well 倒不如;還不如
- broad 廣義的
- generic 一般性的;總稱性的
- headings 標題;首頁文字
- under 在 …名稱下

- weed out 剔除；淘汰
- burst with 塞滿
- chase 追捕；追逐

A reminder 小提醒

「used to」常用來表示過去所習慣做的事物，其後須與不定詞連用且多用在直述句：

> I used to jog 3 miles a day (but I didn't do that anymore).
>
> The young man used to be an excellent student when he was little (but not now anymore).

另外，用來表示習慣的用法還有：

> be used to + V-ing（表示現在的習慣）
>
> I am already used to leaving office late.
>
> The new hire（新進員工）is used to coming early to get a head start.
>
> 新進員工習慣早到提前開始（工作）。
>
> get used to + V-ing（表示未來的習慣）
>
> If you want to prove yourself, you will have to get used to coming in early and leaving late.
>
> 如果你要證明自己，你要習慣早到晚退。

Exercise 練習

利用括弧所提供的字來改寫句子：

❶ Actually I'm not surprised.

(to tell the truth, he doesn't)

❷ This is the third time he's come to me for a missing document.

(twice before, to inquire about)

❸ If you don't know where a document is, it might as well not exist.

(in which file, filed, have been lost)

✸ to tell the truth 老實說

✸ inquire 詢問；調查

Say It Differently 換種說法

 You know, it really burns me up the way he comes rushing in here and say, "Nancy, I want that."

 Believe me, I know exactly how you feel. After a couple of years at my old job I was always getting phone calls from people other than my boss for help on one thing or another.

 Did you do what they wanted?

 Often I didn't feel I could say no. But I consoled myself that the reason they were calling me was because they knew they could depend on me.

Translation 譯文

Nancy　你知道嗎，他衝進來對我說「Nancy 我要這個」的方式真的會激怒我。

Steve　相信我，我完全了解妳的感受。我在之前的公司待了幾年後，我總是接到我老闆以外的人打電話要我幫這幫那的。

Nancy　你有照他們的話做嗎？

Steve　很多次我不覺得我能說不，但我安慰自己他們之所以打電話給我是他們可以依靠我。

* burn one up　激怒某人
* rush in　衝進來
* one thing or another　某事
* console　安慰
* depend on　依賴；依靠

Answer Key 練習解答

❶ To tell the truth, he doesn't surprise me.

❷ He's come to me twice before to inquire about a missing document.

❸ If you don't know in which file a document is filed, it might as well have been lost.

House Cleaning

大清倉

Sample Conversation 範文

(Steve Lee is proposing a house-cleaning in the office.)

 Steve > May I come in?

 Paul > Of course, Steve. My door's always open. So tell me, what's up?

 Steve > I was wondering if you've taken a good look around our office lately. This place is a mess. Paper's flowing out of everybody's drawers and cabinets.

 Paul > I know. Mike Collins has just requested the purchase of additional file cabinets.

 Steve > That's just the point. We don't need more file space to store more paper. What we need is a paper-chase day.

 Paul > Paper-chase day?

 Steve > Yes, everybody should come in on a weekend and throw out old and unnecessary documents, manila folders and files. Reorganize our cabinets and make the place look tidy.

 Paul > Hmm, that's not a bad suggestion. I hate to think how much time we all waste looking for missing files. Where did you get the idea?

 Steve > From International Trading, where I used to work.

Paul Didn't the employees complain about having to come to work on a weekend?

Steve We got an extra day off in the summer. And it was something of a fun event.

 Translation 譯文

（Steve Lee 建議來個辦公室大清倉。）

Steve 我能進來嗎？

Paul 當然，Steve。我的門總是開的，告訴我有什麼事嗎？

Steve 我不知道你最近是否有好好看看我們的辦公室，這地方是一團糟。文件都從所有人的抽屜和檔案櫃中跑出來了。

Paul 我知道，Mike Collins 剛剛才要求購買新檔案櫃。

Steve 這正是問題的所在，我們不需要再買檔案櫃塞更多文件，我們需要的是文件大清掃。

Paul 文件大清掃？

Steve 是的，每個人都該在某個週末進公司把舊的和沒用的文件、信封和檔案丟掉。重新整理我們的檔案櫃並讓整個地方看起來整齊。

Paul 這個建議不錯。我很不希望看見我們為了找不見的文件要花如此多的時間。你從哪裡得來的點子？

Steve 我以前工作的國際貿易公司。

Paul 沒有員工埋怨他們在週末必須工作嗎？

Steve 我們在暑期時多休一天假，而且它也是件好玩的事。

Words & Phrases 詞彙片語

- What's up? 怎麼了？
- take a good look around 好好看看；審視
- lately 最近
- in a mess 亂七八糟；雜亂無序
- flow out 溢出；流出來
- drawer 抽屜
- purchase 購買；採購
- additional 額外的；附加的
- That's just the point 這就是問題的所在
- space 空間
- store 儲存
- throw out 丟掉；否決
- tidy 整齊的；井然的
- hate 討厭；憎恨
- waste 浪費
- complain 埋怨；抱怨
- get a day off 休假一天
- event 活動；事件

A reminder 小提醒

「What's up?」是現代英文中常見的招呼語，除此之外還有：

How's going?

How's life treating you?

What's happening?

傳統的英語見面時用的寒暄語反倒不是那麼流行：

How are you?

How have you been（lately）？

另外，英文中形容詞和副詞雖然有時長相一樣或類似，但用法大不相同：

late 遲到　lately 最近

He came in late for the meeting. 開會時遲到了。

How have you been lately? 最近如何？

high 高　highly 非常

Aim high and reach far! 胸懷壯志力爭上游！

I recommend this restaurant highly. 我非常推薦這家餐廳。

Exercise 練習

利用括弧所提供的字來改寫句子：

❶ I was wondering if you've taken a good look around our office lately.

(take, did you ever)

❷ I hate to think how much time we all waste looking for missing files.

(it bothers me, is lost, trying to locate)

❸ Didn't the employees complain about having to come to work on a weekend?

(any complaints, report, were there)

* ever 曾經
* locate 找出；查看
* report (v.) 報到；報告；報導
* complaint 埋怨（名詞）

☀ Say It Differently 換種說法

 Paul > Back at corporate headquarters we had a rule that you were to leave nothing on your desk when you went home, except for your telephone.

 Steve > That's exactly what I was told to do when I started working here. But it was already pretty much of a dead letter then, and the situation has been deteriorating rapidly ever since.

 Paul > Obviously we can't go on like this. More file cabinets is one thing, but before you know it, they'll be saying we need a bigger office. And with all the way rents in Taipei...

◖ Translation 譯文

 Paul > 我們公司總部有一項規定，當你回家時，除了電話，不能把任何東西留在桌上。

 Steve 這正是我一開始在這裡工作時被告知的，但那時它就是個如同虛設的
規定，而且情況從那時起更是日益惡化。

 Paul 很明顯地，我們不能再如此下去，更多的檔案櫃是一件事，但很快地
就有人會說我們要更大的辦公室。臺北的房租…

✱ headquarters 總部

✱ rule 規則；規定

✱ dead letter 如同虛設的規定；無法投遞的信件

✱ deteriorate （日益）惡化；變壞

✱ rapidly 快速地

✱ obviously 明顯地

✱ go on 繼續（下去）

✱ rent 房租

Answer Key 練習解答

❶ Did you ever take a good look around our office lately?

❷ It bothers me to think how much time is lost trying to locate missing files.

❸ Were there any complaints about having to report to work on a weekend?

A Cluttered Desk Is a Sign of a Cluttered Mind

凌亂的桌子就是腦子凌亂的跡象

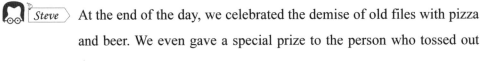

Sample Conversation 範文

(Steve Lee got more than he's bargaining for.)

Steve > At the end of the day, we celebrated the demise of old files with pizza and beer. We even gave a special prize to the person who tossed out the most paper.

Paul > That should encourage him to hoard even more paper for the next time. I'd give an award to someone who comes up with a better central filing system.

Steve > Filing isn't just a clerical function. The managers should also understand how the system works. If it's set up properly, we should be able to retrieve any piece of paper from the office files within three minutes.

Paul > You're right. File retrieval shouldn't be a guessing game. That reminds me, somewhere I read that there's a close correlation between promptability and neat desks.

Steve > Yes, but there's always someone who hates to get rid of paper. When we had a paper-chase day at International Trading, one of my colleagues said, "Just in case we need any of this information in the future, let's make a copy of everything we throw out."

Paul （Laughing）You must be joking.

 Steve I guess he's still there, unless he got buried in a paper avalanche.

 Paul While we're at it, we should also clean out our computer files. Can I make you the project manager, Steve, to work on the details?

 Steve Uh, sure.

Translation 譯文

（Steve Lee 自找煩惱。）

 Steve 到了那天的尾聲時，我們用披薩和啤酒來慶祝老檔案的死亡，我們甚至頒個特別獎給丟掉最多的人。

 Paul 這應該會鼓勵他在下回之前多儲存些紙張，我會把獎給能想出處理中央檔案系統最好方式的人。

 Steve 歸檔不只是職員的工作，經理也該了解系統是如何運作的。如果系統的設置合宜，我們應該能在三分鐘內自辦公室檔案中取出任何一份。

 Paul 你說得對，檔案的取得不該是猜謎遊戲。這剛好提醒我，我在哪讀過說立即採取行動的能力和桌面的整潔有相關性。

 Steve 是的，但總是有人不喜歡丟。當我們在國際貿易公司的文件清掃日時，有個同事居然說要把所有丟掉的東西影印一份以防萬一。

 Paul （笑）你一定是在開玩笑了！

 Steve 除非他已被雪崩般的文件掩埋，不然我想他應該還在公司吧。

 *Paul* 趁我們還沒離題，我們也該清理電腦中的檔案。Steve，我能否讓你當專案經理來處理細節？

 Steve 當然可以。

Words & Phrases 詞彙片語

- clutter 亂糟糟地堆滿
- more than one is bargaining for 和要求不盡相同（通常是較壞的）結果
- celebrate 慶祝
- demise 死亡
- prize 獎賞；獎品
- toss out 丟棄；扔掉
- encourage 鼓勵
- hoard 儲存；珍藏
- award 獎項
- come up with 想出來
- central filing system 中央檔案系統
- clerical 職員的
- function 職責；功能；作用
- work (v.) 發揮功能
- set up 設置；設立；擺設
- properly 適當地
- retrieve 取得；收回
- retrieval retrieve 的名詞
- guessing game 猜謎遊戲
- correlation 相關性
- promptability 能立即採取行動的能力
- neat 乾淨的；很棒的

- get rid of 擺脫；丟掉
- just in case 以防萬一
- buried 被埋在⋯
- avalanche 雪崩；山崩；冰崩
- project mamanger 專案經理
- work on details 處理細節

A reminder 小提醒

「You got what you're bargaining for.」有時為了要更好，我們在工作上少不得會做些建議。建議雖受到認同，但你卻要擔負起執行的責任，這時這句話就能拿來自我解嘲了！

有時，明知結果未必理想，但就是希望能放手一搏。此時，你不妨說：「You got what you paid for.」不管結果如何，要想在長官心目中留下印象，多做事少埋怨應該是正確的選擇吧！

Exercise 練習

利用括弧中所提供的字來改寫句子：

1. We even gave a special prize to the person who tossed out the most paper.
   (presented, discarded, award)
2. I'd give an award to someone who comes up with a better central filing system.
   (more efficient, think up, should be given)
3. There's always someone who hates to get rid of paper.
   (somebody, abhors, dumping)

* present 贈送；提出

* discard 丟棄；拋棄

* efficient 有效率的

* abhor 討厭；憎恨

* dump 傾倒；傾銷

Say It Differently 換種說法

 Paul But you know something, Steve? Most of the Taiwanese company offices I've been to are even worse. Not only are there stacks of paper everywhere, but there seems to be no attention paid to attractive office design.

Steve You're quite right. It would never occur to most traditional managers here that they should spend more money to make their offices look nice. They'd probably think it was wasteful.

Paul It really comes as a shock to someone like me, who always thought that the Taiwanese valued neatness and beauty, when I see the state of people's workplace here.

Translation 譯文

 Paul 但你知道嗎，Steve？大部分我曾去過的臺灣公司更糟，他們不僅到處堆滿文件，他們似乎也不注意辦公室的設計是否吸引人。

 Steve 你說得很對，大多數守舊的管理者都沒想到過如何多花些錢使得他們的辦公室看起來漂亮。他們可能會覺得浪費錢。

 Paul 對像我這個總是覺得臺灣人愛整潔和漂亮的人而言，當我看到這個辦公室的狀態時，實在是件很震驚的事。

✳ But you know something? 你知道嗎？

✳ pay no attention to 不注意；不重視

✳ attractive 吸引人的

✳ traditional 傳統的；典型的

✳ occur to 想起；想到

✳ wasteful 浪費的

✳ value 重視

Answer Key 練習解答

❶ We even presented a special award to the person who discarded the most paper.

❷ An award should be given to someone who can think up a more efficient central filing system.

❸ There's always somebody who abhors dumping paper.

It Can't Be True!

這不是真的！

(Steve Lee is in a state of shock!)

 Nancy   Henry Sherman wants to see you, Steve.

 Steve   Oh, no, not again. Give me a break, will you?

 Nancy   He asked you to meet him in Paul's office.

 Steve   What? In Paul's office? What the hell have I done this time, I wonder?

 Nancy   He didn't tell me what it was about, but he sounded pretty grim, I'm afraid.

 Steve   May as well get it over with, I guess.

 Henry   Steve, thanks for joining us. I've just started explaining to Paul about the situation with Mike Collins. I'll give you a quick recap, but first let me mention that this is in strict confidence. Only the three of us are to know about it at this stage. All right?

 Steve   Sure. What's the story?

 Henry   I've been doing the yearly check of inordinary payments, as required by company policy. In the past I understand that the traditional mid-year and year-end gifts to customers created slight problems at the head office but now they fully appreciate the local customs on that

score. In the course of financial review this time, though, I've discovered that Mike has paid large sums in condolence money – what they call 葬儀 – to customers or their relatives without any proof of actual payment.

Steve〉 Excuse me just a second, Henry, but there's no way you can get a receipt at a funeral.

 Translation 譯文

（Steve Lee 處在一陣震驚中。）

Nancy〉 Steve，Henry Sherman 想要見你。

Steve〉 又來了，饒了我吧，好嗎？

Nancy〉 他要你到 Paul 的辦公室見面。

Steve〉 什麼？在 Paul 的辦公室？我不知我這回又做了什麼？

Nancy〉 他沒告訴我什麼原因，但恐怕聽起來相當嚴重。

Steve〉 希望趕快了結吧！

Henry〉 Steve，謝謝你來。我剛對 Paul 說明 Mike Collins 的狀況，我很快地重述重點，但讓我首先說這是絕對機密，在本階段，只有我們三個知道，好嗎？

Steve〉 好，發生什麼事？

Henry〉 基於公司要求，我在對不尋常付款做年度檢查。我知道以往總公司對我們在年中和歲末送客戶禮物的做法曾有些小問題，但他們現在完全理解這是在地習俗，但在這回財務稽核過程中我發現 Mike 在沒有實際支付證明下支付了大筆喪儀費給客戶或他們的親戚。

Steve 〉 先等一下，Henry，你無法在喪禮拿到收據。

⟨ Words & Phrases 詞彙片語

- a state of 在 … 的狀態
- shock 震驚
- not again 不會再來一次吧
- give me a break 饒了我吧
- what the hell 究竟；到底
- sound 聽來
- grim 嚴厲的；可怕的
- get it over with 做完了事（通常指不愉快但卻非做不可的事）
- quick 快速的
- recap 重述重點
- strict 絕對的；嚴格的
- confidence 機密
- stage 階段；舞臺
- What's the story? 怎麼回事？
- yearly 每年的；一年一次的
- inordinary 不規律的
- payment 付款
- required 被要求的
- mid-year 年中
- year-end 年終
- appreciate 體會；感激；欣賞

● score 論點；得分；樂譜

● in the course of 在 … 的過程中

● financial review 財務稽核

● discover 發現

● sum 總數；金額

● condolence 弔唁；慰問

● funeral 葬禮；喪禮

▌ A reminder 小提醒

「recap」是「recapitulate」的縮寫，意指「重點重複」或「歸納」，英語中有很多字是如這般省去字尾，如：

lab = laboratory 實驗室

high-tech = high technology 高科技

op ed = opposite editorial 與社論相反的其他論述

math = mathematics 數學

condo = condominium 分戶出售的公寓

perks = perquisites 超額收益

sci-fi = science fiction 科幻小說

✎ Exercise 練習

利用括弧所提供的字來改寫句子：

❶ He asked you to meet him in Paul's office.

(he said he wanted, to come to, for a meeting)

❷ He didn't tell me what it was about, but he sounded pretty grim.

(the subject, didn't say, awfully)

❸ Only the three of us are to know about it at this stage.

(I don't want anyone else, at this point in time, share the knowledge)

✱ subject 主題；臣民；學科；理由

✱ awfully 非常地；可怕地

✱ share 向 … 訴說；與 … 分享

✱ knowledge 了解；知識；見聞

☀ Say It Differently 換種說法

 Steve ❯ I wonder why we have to meet in Paul's office. If I've violated one of his myriad rules again, I wish he'd just tell about it instead of calling me on the carpet in front of the boss.

 Nancy ❯ Steve, aren't you forgetting one possibility?

 Steve ❯ What's that?

Nancy ❯ If your conscience is clear, maybe it's not about anything you've done. It could be about some other problem, don't you think?

 Steve ❯ Well, let's hope so.

Translation 譯文

Steve > 我不知道為什麼我們要在 Paul 辦公室碰面，如果我再次違反了他那眾多規定中的一項，我希望他直接告訴我而不要在老闆面前數落我。

Nancy > Steve，你是不是忘了一種可能？

Steve > 是什麼？

Nancy > 如果你自認無愧良心，也許不是和你所做的某事有關。你不覺得可能是他人的麻煩嗎？

Steve > 希望如此。

* violate 違反；侵犯；妨害
* myriad 大量的；無數的
* call...on the carpet 譴責；批評
* in front of 在 …之前
* possibility 可能（性）
* conscience 良知；道德心
* clear 清白的；無罪的

Answer Key 練習解答

❶ He said he wanted you to come to Paul's office for a meeting.

❷ He didn't say what the subject was, but he sounded awfully grim.

❸ I don't want anyone else to share the knowledge at this point in time.

You're Kidding Me!

少來了！

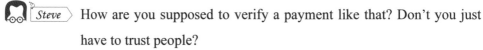

Sample Conversation 範文

(Steve Lee is learning more about the details.)

Steve How are you supposed to verify a payment like that? Don't you just have to trust people?

Henry I quite understand the difficulty. What alerted me to Mike's case was the fact that he's been to eight funerals during the past year and paid up to NT$5,000 each time. I also found out that at least five of the people were either still alive or never existed.

Steve Oh?

Henry I became curious and looked into the other payments related to Mike. One thing I discovered is that he has approved six invoices in the last nine months from a company called Ace Design. The total amount billed to us is about NT$4 million. Unfortunately, this company is also phony.

Paul How did you find that out?

Henry The telephone number listed on the invoice is out of service. And there's no office at the address given. I actually went there myself. It was a condominium registered under the name of none other than Mike's wife.

 Paul Oh, but Henry...How could Mike be so stupid? But isn't all of this only circumstantial evidence so far? It's hard for me to convince myself that he's really involved in any wrongdoing.

 Henry Believe me, it was difficult for me to accept at first too. But to top all that, I got a call this morning from a finance company.

Translation 譯文

（Steve Lee 了解更多細節。）

 Steve 你如何去證實像那樣的支出？你不是就必須信賴人嗎？

 Henry 我相當了解這事的困難度。讓我注意到 Mike 是因為他在去年參加了八個喪禮而且每一場都支付了 5000 元，我也發現這八人中至少有五人還活著或不存在。

 Steve 噢！

Henry 我覺得奇怪並調查其他和 Mike 相關的支出。我發現一件事，他在過去九個月中批准了六張王牌設計公司的發票，我們支付的總額是四百萬新臺幣。很不幸，這家公司也是假的。

 Paul 你是如何發現的？

Henry 列在發票上的電話已暫停服務，上面的地址也沒有任何公司。我還親自去過，那裡是一間登記在 Mike 太太名下的公寓。

Paul 但是 Henry…Mike 怎可能如此笨？但到目前為止這些不都是間接證據嗎？我很難說服自己 Mike 的確涉及任何犯罪。

Henry 相信我，因為一開始我也很難接受。但火上加油的是我今早接到一家財務公司的電話。

Words & Phrases 詞彙片語

- learn about 聽到關於 …；學習
- be supposed to 認為必須；認為 … 有必要
- verify 證實；核對
- trust 信任
- alert 使警覺；使注意
- up to 多達
- alive 活著的；活潑的；有生氣的
- curious 好奇的；求知的
- look into 調查
- relate to 與 … 有關
- approve 核准
- invoice 發票
- unfortunately 不幸地
- phony 假的；欺騙的
- out of service 停止運行；暫停服務
- register 登記
- under the name of 在 … 名下
- no other than 正是
- stupid 愚蠢的
- circumstantial evidence 旁證；間接證據
- so far 到目前為止
- convince 說服；使信服

- involved in 涉及
- wrongdoing 壞事；罪行
- accept 接受
- at first 一開始
- top 超越
- finance company 金融公司

A reminder 小提醒

「alive」是形容詞，但和其他形容詞，如「live」或「living」的用法不同：

> There was a live band performed on stage at the party last night.
>
> 昨晚在宴會上有現場樂團表演。
>
> Not a living soul could be found in the room.
>
> 房內沒有一個人。
>
> The old man was still alive after the heart seizure.
>
> 老人在心臟病發作後依然活著。

一般形容詞多放在修飾對象之前，但若形容詞的第一個字母是 a，如 alike、afraid、ashamed 等，它們的位置必須放在修飾對象之後：

> The boy and his father are alike. 父子很像。

Exercise 練習

利用括弧所提供的字來改寫句子：

❶ How are you supposed to verify a payment like that?

(substantiate, can you possibly)

❷ How did you find that out?

(able, determine)

❸ It was difficult for me to accept at first.

(found it, believe)

✱ substantiate 證實

✱ determine 做出決定；下決心

Say It Differently 換種說法

 Paul Was the design work actually done?

 Steve Some of it seems to have been completed, but it's hard to tell because there's so little information in the file. One thing is for sure that the charges are way out of line.

Paul I can't believe it. Mike just celebrated his 15th anniversary with the company last month.

Henry Computerization and electronic money transfer systems make it easier to succumb to temptation. No one's there to see the look of guilt on your face when you're doing the evil act.

Paul⟩ Often, money is the yardstick by which people measure success and it's a very corrupting gauge.

Translation 譯文

Paul⟩ 設計工作有切實執行嗎？

Steve⟩ 其中一些似乎完成了，但因為檔案中資料很少而很難看得出。有一件事是確定的，那就是收費太高了。

Paul⟩ 我無法相信。Mike 剛在上個月慶祝他加入公司 15 週年呢。

Henry⟩ 電腦化和電子金融轉帳系統讓人容易屈服在誘惑之前，當你做壞事時，沒有人會看到你臉上的罪惡感。

Paul⟩ 人們通常用金錢來衡量成功，但它也是個腐敗的標準。

✱ hard to tell 很難決定

✱ for sure 確定的

✱ way out of line 太過分了

✱ anniversary 週年慶

✱ computerization 電腦化

✱ electronic money 電子錢

✱ transfer 轉移；調動

✱ succumb 屈服

✱ temptation 誘惑

✱ look 神貌；眼神；樣子

✱ guilt 罪惡

✱ evil 罪惡的；品行壞的

✻ act 行為

✻ measure 衡量；測量

✻ corrupting 腐化的

✻ yardstick 衡量標準；價值標準

✻ gauge 標準

Answer Key 練習解答

❶ How can you possibly substantiate a payment like that?

❷ How were you able to determine that?

❸ I found it difficult to believe at first.

All's Goes Well That Does Not End Well
並不是所有有情人到最後都終成眷屬

◯ Sample Conversation 範文

(Steve Lee felt really sorry for Mike Collins.)

 Henry They're asking for a court injunction to seize Mike's salary for a NT$5 million loan on which he hasn't been making the repayment.

 Paul Henry, you ought to talk to Mike and get his side of the story, if he has any. I really hope he has some good explanation for all this.

 Paul How did it go?

 Henry When I faced Mike with what I knew about Ace Design, he admitted it was front for his wife – soon to be his ex-wife, since apparently they're in the process of getting divorced. Anyway, his story was that she actually did what he called "design consultation" for the company but that he was afraid to have her bill the company using her own name, so he had her make up this fictitious corporation, open a bank account in its name, and use her place as its mailing address. But he claimed he had done nothing really wrong.

 Steve How about those fishy condolence money payments?

 Henry When I hit him with those, together with the phone call from the loan outfit, I think he realized the game was up. He said that he would ten-

der his resignation immediately and use his severance allowance to pay off the loan.

 A case like this probably warrants a disciplinary dismissal, but I think I'll let Mike collect his voluntary severance package. Lord knows, he can certainly use the money. I only wish this hadn't happened.

 Don't we all!

Translation 譯文

（Steve Lee 為 Mike Collins 感到婉惜。）

 他們因 Mike 未能還五百萬新臺幣的貸款而要求法院的禁制令來沒收 Mike 的薪水。

 Henry，如果 Mike 有任何解釋，你該和他談談並聽聽他的說法。我真希望他可以好好解釋這些事。

 狀況如何？

 當我就我所知的王牌設計公司的種種與 Mike 對質時，他承認那是他太太的幌子。他們正在辦理離婚，他太太很快就會變成他的前妻了。不管怎樣，他的說法是他太太的確為公司做他所謂的設計諮商但他怕用他太太的名字向公司收費，所以要她編了個虛構的公司，用公司名字開了個銀行戶頭，並用她的住所當郵寄住址，但他堅持自己沒做錯事。

 那些有問題的喪禮悼慰金呢？

 當我用這還有貸款單位的電話去打擊他的要害時，他知道沒戲唱了。他說他會馬上遞辭呈並用他的資遣費來付清貸款。

 像他這樣可能要開除，但我想我會讓 Mike 拿到他的自願離職金。老天

爺清楚他會用到那些錢的。我真希望這事沒發生。

Steve 我們都一樣。

Words & Phrases 詞彙片語

- All's well that does not end well. 原為莎士比亞的劇作「All's well that ends well. 終成眷屬」現在改成反諷的用法。
- court injunction 禁制令
- seize 沒收；占領；奪取
- salary 薪資；薪水
- loan 貸款
- make a repayment 還款
- his side of the story 他的說法
- explanation 說明；解釋
- How did it go? 進行如何？
- admit 承認；准許進入
- front 幌子；前面；前線
- ex-wife 前妻
- apparently 明顯地；表面上地
- in the process of 在 … 的過程中
- get divorced 離婚
- consultation 諮詢；諮商
- make up 捏造；賠償；彌補
- fictitious 虛構的；假裝的
- bank account 銀行帳戶

- mailing address 通信住址

- claim 聲稱；主張

- fishy 可疑的；腥味的

- loan outfit 借貸公司

- the game is up 遊戲結束了

- tender （正式）提出；投標

- resignation 辭職；辭呈

- severance allowance 資遣費；離職津貼

- pay off 付清

- warrant 使 ⋯ 有正當的理由

- disciplinary dismissal 開除

- voluntary 自願的

- severance package 解雇金條款

- Lord knows （只有）天知道

A reminder 小提醒

「Don't we all !」是個感嘆句：

Don't we all wish that this hadn't happened.

和一般感嘆句用「what」或「how」是一樣的道理：

What a shame! 好可惜！
How it ended! 如此下場！

有時其他的表達也有感嘆的意味：

I goofed! 我敗得很慘！

Try harder! 再努力些！

What's that! 究竟是怎麼回事啊！

所以，英語句型可說是千變萬化！

Exercise 練習

利用括弧所提供的字來改寫句子：

❶ You ought to talk to Mike and get his side of the story.

(for, why don't, ask Mike)

❷ Apparently they're in the process of getting divorced.

(seem to be, splitting up)

❸ He can certainly use the money.

(I'm sure, needs)

✱ split up 分手；分裂

Say It Differently 換種說法

 Paul Henry, I certainly owe you a big thank-you for getting to the bottom of this so efficiently.

 Henry Oh, it's nothing. I was just doing my job.

 Paul ⟩ Maybe so, but doing it very well. I realize that being an accountant isn't the best way to win friends in the company under any circumstances.

 Henry ⟩ But I truly enjoy my profession, and that makes it a lot easier.

Translation 譯文

 Paul ⟩ Henry，我應該因你有效地深入調查真相而向你深深致謝。

 Henry ⟩ 沒什麼，我只不過盡自己的本分。

 Paul ⟩ 也許是盡本分，但本分盡得非常好。我知道在任何狀況下，當會計不是在公司裡贏得朋友的最佳之道。

 Henry ⟩ 但我喜歡我的工作，這樣讓事情變得容易多了。

✳ owe 欠；歸功於

✳ the bottom of 查明真相

✳ doing one's job 盡本分

✳ win 獲得；贏得；說服

✳ under any circumstance 不管在什麼情況下

Answer Key 練習解答

❶ Why don't you ask Mike for his side of the story?

❷ They seem to be in the process of splitting up.

❸ I'm sure he needs the money.

First in, last out

最早到，最晚走

Sample Conversation 範文

(Steve Lee is literally living in his office.)

 Paul　Steve! You scared the daylight out of me. I can't believe you're still here. Do you realize it's 11 o'clock? Time to go home and get some sleep.

 Steve　Sorry to surprise you. I heard a noise over here and thought I should check it out. But tell me, what's a nice guy like you doing in a place like this? Still a bit early for a power breakfast meeting, isn't it?

 Paul　Very funny. No, actually I was at a party and discovered that I left key to my apartment in my office. So I stopped by to pick it up. I had no idea you were still at work.

 Steve　Well, there's so much to do around here. And I still haven't caught up from my last business trip. Work gets piled up while I'm away and after I'm back there seems to be a never-ending stream of paper crossing my desk. I was just working on a status report turned in by a brand manager. I wish he had done a better job organizing the material and putting it in perspective. I can't make head or tail of it.

 Paul　You know, Steve, I'm afraid you're turning into an incurable workaholic. You certainly exhibit the symptoms.

 Steve　What symptoms?

 Paul　Recently your whole life seems to be just work and instant noodles. Don't let work become an end in itself or a way of fooling yourself and others into believing that you're indispensable. I'm really worried about you, Steve.

 Steve　Are you trying to tell me that I'm dispensable?

 Paul　We're all dispensable. You, me, everybody.

Translation　譯文

（Steve Lee 就差沒住在公司。）

 Paul　Steve！你嚇死我了，我不敢相信你還在這裡。你知道現在已經 11 點了嗎？該回家睡覺囉！

 Steve　抱歉嚇到你，我聽到這裡有聲響覺得該查查看，但告訴我你這種正常的人來這種地方幹嘛？明天的主管早餐會報還早，不是嗎？

 Paul　很好笑，我在一個聚會裡發現我把我公寓的鑰匙放在辦公室，所以我順道來拿。我不知道你還在工作。

 Steve　在這裡有好多事要做，而我連上回出差的結果都還沒搞定。我不在時工作一直累積，回來後又有無止境的公文往我桌上排山倒海而來。我剛在弄一位品牌經理交來的工作進度報告，我希望他能把資料通盤組織的工作做得精確些。我已分不出頭尾了。

 Paul　你知道嗎，Steve，恐怕你變成了無可救藥的工作狂了。你的確顯現出某些症狀。

 Steve　什麼症狀？

 Paul 最近你的生活裡只有工作和泡麵，別讓工作變成生活目標，也別讓你
自己和他人誤以為你是不可或缺的工具。我真的很擔心你，Steve。

 Steve 你想告訴我我是可有可無的？

 Paul 你、我、所有人，我們都是可有可無的。

Words & Phrases 詞彙片語

- literally 實在地；不加誇張地；字面上地
- scare the daylight out of 嚇死人了
- noise 聲音；噪音
- check out 檢查
- power breakfast meeting 主管早餐會報
- pick up 拿；拾起；接機；學會；逮捕
- catch up 趕上
- pile up 累積；增多；（車輛）連環碰撞
- never-ending 永無休止
- stream of 一連串；趨勢
- cross 穿越；橫跨；相交叉
- work on 從事於；忙於
- status report 現況報告；工作進度表
- brand manager 品牌經理
- put...in perspective 正確且通盤地
- make head or tail of 明白；了解
- turn into 變成
- workaholic 工作狂

- exhibit 顯出；陳列；展示
- symptom 徵兆；症狀
- instant noodle 速食麵；泡麵
- end 終點；目標
- in itself 本身；本質上
- make fool of oneself 做傻事；鬧笑話
- indispensable 不可或缺的
- dispensable 非必要的

▌◀ A reminder 小提醒

英文裡有很多字彙是在字尾加上些字根而形成新字，「-holic」是「狂」，指沉迷於某事的人：

beerholic 嗜喝啤酒的人

colaholic 愛喝可樂的人

movie-holic 喜歡看電影的人

teleholic 看電視上癮的人

carboholic 嗜喝汽水的人

alcoholic 酒精中毒的人

若不喜歡害怕或恐懼，只要在字尾加上「-phobia」即可：

autophobia 害怕獨處的人

claustrophobia 有幽閉恐懼症的人

dentophobia 怕牙醫的人

ergophobia 怕工作的人

Exercise 練習

利用括弧所提供的字來改寫句子：

1 I had no idea you were still at work.

(working, never knew)

2 I was just working on a status report truned in by a brand manager.

(have been busy, reviewing, product manager)

3 Are you trying to tell me that I'm dispensable?

(suggest, can be dispensed with, do you mean)

Say It Differently 換種說法

 Steve I really don't mind traveling on business. It gives me a chance to meet new people and go to new places. But I hate coming back to a desk loaded with a couple of weeks' worth of work to catch up on.

 Paul How about your wife? I don't suppose she likes being left on her own while you're gone.

 Steve She's never complained. Since I'm practically never home in the evening, breakfast is the only time she sees me anyway. And when I'm not there she can sleep late and let the kids look after themselves.

 Paul Oh, I'm sure she misses you. She probably just doesn't think you'd respond if she said so.

Translation 譯文

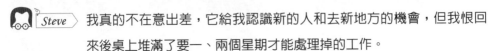

Steve 我真的不在意出差，它給我認識新的人和去新地方的機會，但我恨回來後桌上堆滿了要一、兩個星期才能處理掉的工作。

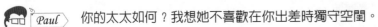

Paul 你的太太如何？我想她不喜歡在你出差時獨守空閨。

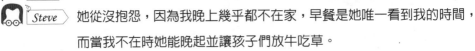

Steve 她從沒抱怨，因為我晚上幾乎都不在家，早餐是她唯一看到我的時間，而當我不在時她能晚起並讓孩子們放牛吃草。

Paul 我確信她想你，她可能以為如果她說了你也不會有回應。

* loaded with 充滿了；富有的；喝醉的
* worth of 數量或價值
* on one's own 獨自一人
* practically 實際上；幾乎
* sleep late 晚起
* look after 照顧
* miss 思念；錯過
* respond 回應

Answer Key 練習解答

❶ I never knew you were still working.

❷ I have been busy reviewing a status report turned in by a product manager.

❸ Do you mean to suggest that I can be dispensed with?

No One Is Indispensable

沒有人是不可少的

Sample Conversation 範文

(Steve Lee realized that anyone can be replaced.)

Paul The way we used to put it in the States is that you should dispense with somebody as soon as they start getting indispensable. It's not healthy to have a situation where the absence of a single person can make the whole office fall apart.

Steve Even so, I'd rather be a workaholic than an alcoholic.

Paul Both work and alcohol can be fine in moderation. But you can get addicted to either, and it's dangerous for you if you do.

Steve Well, I've been raised in the Taiwanese tradition, which values diligence and frugality. Hard work is the highest virtue of all, as idleness is considered a sin.

Paul Yes, I understand that. But hard work is one thing; being a workaholic is another.

Steve Should I say I'm sorry?

Paul Don't get me wrong, Steve. I'm not saying I don't appreciate your work. But hard workers get their jobs done; workaholics get done by their jobs. When's the last time you took a vacation?

Steve I haven't had time since I started here.

Paul See what I mean? In English we have a proverb, "All work and no play makes Jack a dull boy." You have a fine personality, with lots of drive and energy, but you're going to burn yourself out unless you let up a little bit.

 Steve But I've seen executives in this company who take their jobs even more seriously than I do. It's all they seem to think about even when they're socializing.

 Paul Oh, I know those types. I used to have a boss like that.

 Translation 譯文

（Steve Lee 理解到任何人都能被替代。）

 Paul 以前在美國我們習慣在某人變得不可或缺時替換他。一個人的缺席使得整個辦公室崩潰不是好事。

 Steve 就算如此，我情願當工作狂也不要當酒鬼。

Paul 工作和酒精若適量都是好事，但你會對其中一個上癮，而上癮是很危險的。

Steve 我是在重視勤奮和節省的臺灣傳統中長大的，辛勤工作是最高的美德，而懶惰則是一種罪惡。

Paul 我了解，但辛勤工作是一回事，工作狂又是另一件事。

Steve 我該說對不起嗎？

Paul 別會錯意，Steve。我不是說我不欣賞你的工作，辛勤工作的人把事做好，而工作狂則被事了結。你上回休假是什麼時候？

 Steve 我從在這裡工作開始就沒休過。

Paul > 了解我的意思了吧？英語中有句俗話：「只有工作沒有娛樂的人生是黑白的」，你有個好的人格特質，有很多的動力和精力，但除非你把腳步放慢，否則你會油盡燈枯。

Steve > 但我看到公司裡有比我還重視工作的高階主管，就連他們在社交時還是想著工作。

Paul > 噢，我知道那種類型的，我以前有個老闆就是如此。

Words & Phrases 詞彙片語

- replace 替換；取代
- as soon as 一…就…
- absence 缺席；缺勤；缺乏；心不在焉
- single 單一的
- fall apart 崩潰；散開
- in moderation 適量的
- get addicted to 對…上癮
- tradition 傳統；慣例
- value 重視；估價
- diligence 勤勉；勤奮
- frugality 節儉；樸素
- virtue 美德；價值；長處
- idleness 懶惰；閒散；安逸
- consider 認為；考慮
- sin 惡行；過錯；可恥的事
- get someone wrong 誤會他人

- get done by 終結;為 … 解決掉
- take a vacation 度假;休假
- proverb 諺語;俗語
- dull 遲鈍的;單調的;枯燥的
- personality 個性;性格
- drive 驅動力;駕車旅遊
- energy 精力;能源
- burn out 燒光;筋疲力竭
- let up 放輕;變慢
- executive 主管階級
- seriously 認真地;嚴肅地
- socialize 聯誼;參與社交

A reminder 小提醒

「another」是英語中常見的代名詞,用法如下:

O	O	
one	the other	
O	O	O
one	another	the other
O	OOO	
one	the others	
OOO	OOO	
some	the others/the rest	

如果在很多事物中強調另外的一個，就必須用 another：

I don't like this hat, please show me another.

我不喜歡這頂帽子，請拿另外一頂給我看。

Exercise 練習

利用括弧所提供的字來改寫句子：

❶ I'd rather be a workaholic than an alcoholic.

(prefer being, to being)

❷ Hard work is one thing; being a workaholic is another.

(working hard, not the same as)

❸ I haven't had time to since I started here.

(too busy, joined this company)

✽ prefer...to... 喜歡…；勝過…

✽ join 加入；參與；結合

Say It Differently 換種說法

 Steve Besdies, even if I took a vacation, what would I do? My kids are busy studying, and when they're not, they'd rather be with their friends than go somewhere with me.

 Paul Couldn't just you and your wife take a trip by yourselves? I should

think it would be a nice change of pace for both of you.

 Steve ⟩ I suppose we could, but traveling is so expensive.

 Paul ⟩ Oh, Steve, you're impossible! I'm sure you can afford it. If not, you could save the money by cutting back a bit on your after-hour bar crawling.

 Steve ⟩ Well, I suppose so.

Translation 譯文

 Steve ⟩ 而且就算我休個假,我能做什麼?我的孩子們都忙著上課,當他們不上課時,他們情願和他們的朋友出去玩也不要和我一起出去。

 Paul ⟩ 你就不能和你太太兩人去旅行嗎?我覺得你們兩個改變一下(生活)步調也好。

 Steve ⟩ 我想我們能,但旅行好貴。

 Paul ⟩ Steve,你真是不可理喻!我相信你負擔得了的,如果不行,你可以從你下班後續攤喝酒費用中省出來。

 Steve ⟩ 我想我可以吧!

✳ would rather 寧願
✳ take a trip 旅行
✳ by oneself 單獨
✳ change of pace 改變習慣;變換節奏
✳ expensive 昂貴
✳ impossible 不可理喻
✳ cut back on 減少;縮減

✱ bar-crawling 去一家接著一家的酒吧喝酒

Answer Key 練習解答

❶ I prefer being a workaholic to being an alcoholic.

❷ Working hard is not the same as being a workaholic.

❸ I've been too busy since I joined this company.

A Happy Man Is a Productive Man
快樂的人才是有生產力的人

 Sample Conversation 範文

(Steve Lee finally realizes the way of working hard.)

 Paul I remember the time we were attending the annual management meeting at a hotel in Florida a few years ago. The last evening there was a party for the whole group in the hotel ballroom. I had been trying for days to get my boss to give me some time to talk about my business plans for the following year, but he was always too busy. So I walked over to his table, apologizing for interrupting, and asked if I could ride back on the plane with him the next day so we could discuss my plans then. He said he already had an in-flight meeting set up and told me to pull up a chair and talk to him right then and there. So there I was in my party gear giving him an impromptu presentation without so much as a flipchart. And all the while his wife was giving me these hostile looks. Believe me, it was murder.

 Steve Who was that, anybody I know?

 Paul No, he left the company a couple of years ago, but I'm sure he's still spreading stress wherever he goes.

 Steve Am I "spreading stress" too?

 Paul Whether you care to admit it or not, I'd say you are. You're probably

also breeding some resentment if you want others to work like you. You ought to learn how to manage your energy, to pace yourself and maintain a good psychological balance. You should also delegate more.

 Steve : I guess you may be right.

 Paul : Anyway, let's get out of here. And tomorrow I want you to promise to spend the evening with your family for a change.

 Steve : Yes, sir.

Translation 譯文

（Steve Lee 終於知道什麼叫工作狂了。）

 Paul : 我記得幾年前在佛羅里達參加年度管理會議的那時，最後一晚是在大宴會廳裡為整個團體所舉行的聚會。我已經試了好多天要讓我老闆給我點時間來說說我明年的業務計畫，但他總是沒時間。所以我走到他的桌前打斷他，向他致歉後接著問他我是否第二天能和他一起搭飛機，如此才能和他討論我的計畫。他說他已經安排好了機上會議並要我拉張椅子就地和他談，所以我穿著宴會裝，沒有任何參考配圖，就給他來個即席簡報。同時，他太太的眼神充滿敵意。相信我，那真是如坐針氈。

 Steve : 那是誰，我認識嗎？

 Paul : 不，他幾年前離開公司了，但我確定他一定是去哪兒，就在哪散播壓力。

 Steve : 我也在散播壓力嗎？

 Paul : 不管你願不願意承認，我覺得你有，如果你想要別人和你有一樣的工

作態度的話，你也會招致怨恨。你該學習如何妥善運用你的精力，去調整你的步調和維持良好的心理平衡，你也該充分授權。

 Steve > 我想你可能是對的。

 Paul > 不管怎樣，我們離開這裡。我要你答應我明天晚上你會改變一下，花點時間和家人相處。

 Steve > 遵命！

Words & Phrases 詞彙片語

- productive （有）生產力的
- the way of …之道
- attend 出席；參加；上（課／學）
- annual 一年一次的；全年的
- ballroom 大（舞）廳
- for days 好幾天
- following year 下年度；來年
- ride back 回程
- then 那時
- in-flight 飛行中
- pull up 拉（把椅子）
- then and there 當時當地；立即
- gear 工具；設備；裝置
- impromptu 即席的；臨時的；無準備的
- without so much as 甚至連…都沒有
- flipchart （配套）掛圖

- hostile 懷敵意的；敵對的
- looks 眼神；樣子；長相
- murder 極艱難／沮喪的經歷；謀殺
- a couple of （英）兩個；（美）幾個
- spread 傳播；散發
- stress 壓力
- breed 繁殖；養育；產生；導致
- resentment 憤恨；不滿
- manage 管理
- pace 調整步伐
- maintain 維持；保持
- psychological 心理的
- balance 平衡；均衡
- delegate 授權；委派（代表）
- for a change 變化一下

A reminder 小提醒

「attend」如果是當及物動詞用，意思不同於當不及物動詞時：

I get up early to attend the company breakfast meeting.

我為了出席公司早餐會報早起。

I have something else to attend to.

我另外有事要處理。

而英語動詞片語若其後所加的介系詞改變，意思也會不一樣：

I applied for the admission of a training program.

我申請參加了一個訓練計畫。

I am going to apply this new discovery to other fields.

我要把新發現應用到其他領域。

Exercise 練習

利用括弧所提供的字來改寫句子：

❶ His wife was giving me these hostile looks.

(looking at, angry expression)

❷ He left the company a couple of years ago.

(stopped working for, two or three)

❸ Whether you care to admit it or not, I'd say you are.

(like it, the truth is)

✽ expression 表情；表示；表達

Say It Differently 換種說法

Paul What really burned me up about that man was the way he would make you feel lazy if you didn't work as hard as he did.

Steve I suppose he didn't take vacations either.

 Paul No, actually he took at least three weeks every summer. He had a place on the coast in Maine, and he used to go down there.

 Steve That must have been a sort of vacation for you too.

 Paul It would have been, except that he would call in once, sometimes twice, a day.

Translation 譯文

 Paul 那人讓我生氣的真正原因是如果我不像他一樣努力工作我就是懶惰。

 Steve 我想他也不休假。

 Paul 不,實際上他每年夏天都休三個星期的假。他在緬因州海邊有個地方而且他也習慣到那裡去。

 Steve (他不在) 對你也是休假了。

 Paul 算是,只不過他每天都會打一次,有時兩次電話。

* burn up 發怒;燒毀
* lazy 懶惰
* Maine 美國緬因州
* sort 某種;不尋常 (的事物)
* twice 兩次;兩倍

Answer Key 練習解答

❶ His wife was looking at me with an angry expression.

❷ He stopped working for the company two or three years ago.

❸ Whether you like it or not, the truth is you are.

Kick the Habit for Good

徹底戒除惡習

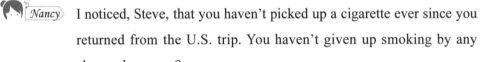

Sample Conversation 範文

(Steve Lee is finally kicking the habit of smoking.)

Nancy I noticed, Steve, that you haven't picked up a cigarette ever since you returned from the U.S. trip. You haven't given up smoking by any chance, have you?

Steve Matter of fact, I have. And you should too, Nancy. It's so easy to stop smoking. I've done it a thousand times – but this time it's for good.

Nancy I started smoking to reduce my weight and now I'm totally addicted to nicotine. But it's my only vice, so...

Steve You really ought to try. The only way to stop smoking is to just stop – no ifs, ands, or buts.

Nancy But I'm trying. I've decided to cut down to only one cigarette...

Steve A day?

Nancy No. At a time. But what made you quit?

Steve After 20 years of smoking, I finally realized how much harm I was doing to myself. Did you know, Nancy, that each cigarette you somke shortens your life by five and a half minutes? And that a 25-year-old person who smokes two packs a day – which is probably what you are – has only a 50 percent chance of living to be 65?

Translation 譯文

（Steve Lee 總算戒菸了。）

Nancy： Steve，我注意到你從美國回來後就沒有再拿起一根菸，你不可能戒菸了吧，有嗎？

Steve： 實際上我是戒了，妳也該戒。Nancy，戒菸不難，我已經戒了一千次了，但這次是來真的。

Nancy： 我開始抽菸是為了減肥而現在我是完全對尼古丁上癮了。但這是我唯一的惡習⋯。

Steve： 妳真的該試試，唯一停止抽菸的方法是說停就停，沒有理由沒有藉口。

Nancy： 但我正在試，我決定把吸菸的量減到一支⋯

Steve： 每天一支？

Nancy： 不，每次。但是什麼讓你戒菸？

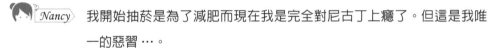
Steve： 在抽菸抽了 20 年後，我終於了解到我對自己造成多大的傷害，妳知道嗎，妳每抽一支菸就會減少妳五又二分之一分鐘的壽命？一個像妳一樣每天抽兩包菸的 25 歲的人，只有 50% 的機會活到 65 歲？

Words & Phrases 詞彙片語

- etiquette 禮儀；禮節；禮數
- kick the habit of 戒除⋯的習慣
- notice 注意；通知；留意
- ever since 自從
- give up 放棄；讓出；停止

- by any chance 或許；可能；萬一
- matter of fact 實際上；其實
- for good 永遠；永久
- reduce 減少；降低；簡化
- weight 體重；重量
- nicotine 尼古丁
- vice 惡習；缺點；惡癖
- no ifs, ands or buts 別為自己找理由或藉口
- cut down 削減；縮短
- at a time 一次
- quit 中斷；停止；辭職
- realize 了解；意識到；實現
- harm 損害；傷害；危害
- shorten 變短；減少
- pack 包；捆；包裹；背包

▌◀ A reminder 小提醒

英語中有時常會引經據典，用古人的說詞或家喻戶曉的雋語來加強想傳達的訊息。
「To quit somking is easy; I've done it a thousdand time.」本是美國幽默作家馬
克吐溫的名言，實際上是一種反諷的用法：戒菸真的不易！

另一句常為人引用的名句是出自莎士比亞的劇作〈哈姆雷特〉中：「To be or not
to be; that's the question.」該句本意在於感嘆人在生死間所面臨的抉擇和掙扎，
但現在多以詼諧的方式引用，某位過胖且正在節食中的男子，站在炸雞排的攤位
前，明知不該吃但仍覬覦那剛自鍋中撈出的誘惑！此時，他不禁說：「To eat or

not to eat; that's the question !」

多看文學作品，多讀神話、傳說。英文的口語表達和文字敘述中很多的資訊是來自非語言層面，所以光是靠知識還不夠，常識更是提升英語能力不可或缺的。

Exercise 練習

利用括弧所提供的字來改寫句子：

❶ You haven't picked up a cigarette ever since you returned from the U.S. trip.

(smoked, your return)

❷ The only way to stop smoking is just to stop.

(be, a non-smoker, just not to smoke)

❸ I finally realized how much harm I was doing to myself.

(damage, causing to, figured out)

✱ non-somker 不吸菸者

    non-smoking area 禁菸區

✱ damage 傷害；損害

✱ cause 導致；引起

Say It Differently 換種說法

Nancy   If I'm deprived of the pleasure of smoking, I don't want to live to be 65.

Steve   I understand how you feel. But there's one thing I'm sure about now. My wife can't nag me anymore. Every time there was something

wrong with me, she used to say that I should stop smoking. She said
that when I broke my leg last year.

 Nancy Even though we're doing something perfectly legal, we smokers are
often discriminated against. In the U.S. drug abuse is a much more serious problem in the workplace.

Translation 譯文

 Nancy 如果剝奪了我抽菸的樂趣，我不想活到 65 歲。

 Steve 我能理解妳的想法，但現在有件事我能確定，我太太不能再嘮叨我了。
每回我不舒服，她總是說我該停止抽菸，我去年腿斷時她就是這麼說的。

 Nancy 雖然我們做的事是完全合法，我們抽菸者常受到歧視，在美國工作場
所的藥物濫用遠比抽菸來得嚴重。

* deprive 剝奪；使⋯喪失⋯

* pleasure 樂趣；快樂；娛樂

* nag 埋怨；找碴；困擾

* even though 即使；儘管

* perfectly 完全地；理想地

* legal 合法的；法定的；法律的

* often 時常；通常

* discriminate 歧視；區別

* against 反對；逆

* drug 藥物；藥劑；毒品

* abuse 濫用；虐待；辱罵

✽ workplace 工作場所；職場

Answer Key 練習解答

❶ You haven't smoked a cigarette ever since your return from the U.S.

❷ The only way to be a non-smoker is just not to smoke.

❸ I finally figured out how much damage I was causing to myself.

The Smokers Are in the Minority!

抽菸的人變少了！

Sample Conversation 範文

(Why Steve Lee had quitted smoking.)

 Nancy So you are serious this time.

 Steve Yes, sir. I've thrown away my ashtrays and lighters and I'm going to put up one of these "Thank you for not smoking" signs in my office.

 Nancy Then I'll have to find my "Vice is nice" sign. I guess I'm in the minority, though. Smoking is down considerably everywhere.

 Steve You said it. Smokers are a dying breed. And I discovered during my trip to the States that smokers are really discriminated against in restaurants, airports, hotels, offices, and everywhere. You're literally abused if you smoke in public places. And now there are anti-smoking laws.

 Nancy I don't understand those laws. Smoking is really a matter of personal choice. It shouldn't be regulated by law. Law-enforcement officers should be after the guys who took your bag, not after me.

 Steve At a convention I attended in the States, I saw a man light up a cigarette and immediately the woman sitting next to him screamed, "For Christ's sake, put out that cigarette. The smoke will kill me." The man gave her a dirty look and said, "What gives you the right to order me

around? It doesn't say 'No smoking' anywhere."

Translation 譯文

（Steve Lee 戒菸的原因。）

> *Nancy*　所以這回你是當真的。
>
> *Steve*　是的，長官。我把我的菸灰缸和打火機都丟掉了，而且我會在我辦公室裡張貼一張禁菸的告示。
>
> *Nancy*　那麼我就得找出我的「罪惡是美」的標示，我想我是少數民族了。抽菸在每個地方都變少了。
>
> *Steve*　沒錯，吸菸者是瀕臨絕跡的物種，我在美國的時候發現，在餐廳、機場、旅館、辦公室以及任何地方，抽菸的人都受到歧視。如果妳在公共場合抽菸，妳的確會受到辱罵，而且現在有禁菸法。
>
> *Nancy*　我不管法律，抽菸實際上是個人選擇，不該用法律來約束。執法人員應該去抓搶包包的人而不是我。
>
> *Steve*　我在美國參加的一場大會中，我看到一個人點菸，坐在他旁邊的女子立即大叫：「幫幫忙！把菸熄掉，煙會殺了我。」那人給了女子厭惡的表情說：「誰給妳權力來指使我的？又沒有禁菸的標誌。」

Words & Phrases 詞彙片語

- in the minority　少數
- throw away　拋棄；浪費
- ashtray　菸灰缸

- lighter 打火機

- put up 張貼；舉起；建造

- sign 符號；記號；暗號；預兆

- in the minority 屬少數派

- abuse 辱罵；侮辱

- literally 實際地

- considerably 相當；非常

- You said it 你說得沒錯

- dying breed 瀕臨絕跡的物種

- anti-smoking law 禁菸法

- choice 選擇

- regulate 控制；管理；調節；規範

- law-enforcement officer 執法人；警察

- after 追求；搜尋

- guy 傢伙

- convention 會議；公約；習俗

- light up 點菸；照亮

- scream 尖叫

- for Christ's sake 看在老天份上

- put out 熄滅；生產；發布

- dirty look 面部的厭惡表情

- right 權力

- order...around 指使；命令

A reminder 小提醒

就像「quit smoking」一樣，下列這些動詞後面都要用動名詞：

acknowledge, admit, advise, advocate, allow, anticipate, appreciate, avoid, complete, consider, contemplate, defer, delay, deny, detest, discuss, dislike, dread, enjoy, ensure, escape, evade, excuse, facilitate, fancy, favor, finish, forbid, forgive, imagine, include, keep, loathe, mention, mind, miss, pardon, permit, practice, postpone, practice, prevent, prohibit, propose, recollect, report, resent, renounce, resist, risk, suggest, tolerate, understand

Exercise 練習

利用括弧所提供的字來改寫句子：

❶ Smoking is down considerably everywhere.

(in, a sharp drop, the number of smokers)

❷ Law-enforcement officers should be after the guys who took your bag, not after me.

(more concerned about, police department, than about)

❸ What gives you the right to order me around?

(push me, who do you think)

✳ sharp 大幅的；猛烈的

* drop 下降；落下
* concern about 關心；顧慮
* police department 警察局
* push 推；逼迫；施壓

Say It Differently 換種說法

> **Nancy** Does cigarette smoke really endanger non-smokers?

> **Steve** I've read the report that non-smoking wives of smokers have a higher risk of lung cancer, but I haven't seen any conclusive evidence. Why don't you like laws against public smoking?

> **Nancy** It's a waste of law-enforcement time. Laws may be appropriate to regulate smoking in dangerous situations, like at filling stations, but they're unnecessary when good judgment and common courtesy prevail. Most smokers can determine how, when and where they may smoke.

Translation 譯文

> **Nancy** 香菸的煙真的會對不吸菸的人有危險嗎？

> **Steve** 我讀過吸菸者不抽菸的太太有較高的致癌率的報告，但我沒看到任何確實的證據。妳為何不喜歡禁止公眾場合吸菸的法律？

> **Nancy** 浪費執法時間，法律規定在危險的地方，像加油站不能抽菸是合宜的，但如果大家都具有好的判斷能力和禮貌的話，實在是沒必要。多數吸菸者都能判定抽菸的場合、時間和地點。

✳ endanger 危及；使…遭到危險

✳ risk 危險；風險

✳ lung cancer 肺癌

✳ conclusive 決定性的；確實的；最終的

✳ evidence 證據；跡象

✳ a waste of time 浪費時間

✳ appropriate 適當的；合宜的

✳ dangerous 危險的

✳ filling station 加油站

✳ judgment 判斷；判決

✳ common 一般的；普通的

✳ courtesy 禮貌；禮儀

✳ prevail 聲張；占優勢

✳ determine 決定；判定；限定

Answer Key 練習解答

❶ There is a sharp drop in the number of smokers everywhere.

❷ The police department should be more concerned about the guy who took your bag than about me.

❸ Who do you think you are to push me around?

At Least Try to Keep Your Job!

就算爲了保住工作吧！

 Sample Conversation 範文

(Steve Lee tries to talk Nancy into quitting smoking.)

 Steve Then the lady went, "Don't you know passive smoke is a cause of serious disease among non-smokers? Put that thing out or get out of here." But the man suggested in a nasty tone that she ought to be the one to leave if she was so concerned. She did but they both made such a spectacle of themselves. The moral of this story is that, these days, where there's smoke there's fire.

 Nancy Seriously, it's mostly a matter of etiquette. If somking really disturbed her, she should have turned to the man and asked in a polite and pleasant tone, "Do you mind terribly waiting to smoke later?" he most likely would have obliged. Incidentally, Steve, I've heard on the grapevine that several heavy smokers in head office were fired recently. Is that true?

 Steve Yes, I've heard that rumor too. It probably is true. In a corporate culture like ours, everybody is suppoed to be bright and healthy. Smoking is considered a sign of personal weakness and even low intelligence. Increasingly, they're being reprimanded, passed over for promotions and even dismissed in the U.S.

Nancy No matter what you tell me, I intend to continue smoking.

Steve Sure, if that's your personal preference. But, Nancy, would you want your children to grow up to be smokers?

Nancy You really got me there. I guess my answer is "no."

Translation 譯文

（Steve Lee 繼續勸 Nancy 戒菸。）

Steve 那位女子又繼續：「你不知道二手菸是造成不吸菸者嚴重疾病的原因嗎？把那玩意放下或離開這裡。」但那人用一種惡劣的語調暗示如果她那麼在意，她才是該離開的人。她離開但他們兩個人讓自己出大糗。這個故事的教訓是在現代只要有煙就會有火（爆）。

Nancy 正經點！這大部分都和禮儀有關。如果抽菸的確讓她感到困擾，她該轉向那人用有禮且悅耳的語調問他能否等下再抽，他很可能會答應。對了，Steve，我聽到總公司開除了幾位老菸槍的傳聞。是真的嗎？

Steve 是的，我也聽到謠言，可能是真的，在像我們這種公司的文化中，每個人都該是活潑健康的。抽菸被視為是個人的弱點甚至於是低智商。在美國，越來越多抽菸的人受到申誡，升遷時被跳過，甚至被資遣。

Nancy 不管你怎麼說，我決定繼續抽菸。

Steve 如果那是妳個人喜好，抽吧！但是 Nancy 妳想要妳小孩長大後變成吸菸者嗎？

Nancy 你問倒我了，我想我的答案是不。

Words & Phrases 詞彙片語

- talk someone into 說服某人做某事
- passive smoke 二手菸
- disease 疾病;弊端
- suggest 暗示;建議
- nasty 令人不愉快的;惡劣的;下賤的
- tone 語氣;語調
- ought to 應該,宜
- spectacle 奇觀;表演;場面
- moral 寓意;教訓
- where there's smoke there's fire 無風不起浪。「smoke」可當香菸也可當煙,此為雙關語(pun)的最佳例證。
- disturb 妨礙;擾亂
- turn to 轉向;致力於
- polite 有禮貌的;殷勤的
- oblige 答應⋯的要求;迫使
- incidentally 順便一提
- on the grapevine 道聽塗說
- several 幾個;數個
- heavy smoker 菸癮很大的人
- recent 最近的
- rumor 謠言;謠傳
- corporate culture 公司文化

- bright 活潑的；鮮明的；愉快的
- weakness 弱點；軟弱
- intelligence 智慧；理解力；情報
- increasingly 越來越多地
- reprimand 懲處；訓斥
- pass over 忽視；置之不理
- promotion 升遷；促銷；提升
- dismiss 遣散；解散；打發走
- intend 打算
- preference 喜愛；偏愛
- You got me there 你把我難倒了；你問倒我了

A reminder 小提醒

「pun」一語雙關是英語裡常用到的一種修辭方法，如在上段範文中所出現的「No ifs, ands or buts.」也可以改成「No ifs, ands or butts.」此處的 butt 發音同 but 但是可解釋為菸蒂！

英語大師胡適先生生前擔任抗戰時期駐美大使時，美國媒體問到日本侵華一事，胡先生回答：「A bull in china shop.」以蠻牛 bull 代替日本軍閥的蠻橫，以 china 一語雙關：又是瓷器店，又是中國！隔日美國各大媒體轉載，間接替中國的堅忍抗戰做最好的宣傳。

Exercise 練習

利用括弧所提供的字來改寫句子：

❶ Put that thing out or get out of here.

（your cigarette, extinguish, leave）

❷ I've heard on the grapevine that several heavy smokers were fired recently.

（let go, in recent weeks, a rumor）

❸ No matter what you tell me, I intend to continue smoking.

（keep on, whatever）

 extinguish 熄滅；破滅；消失

 let go 放手；放開；釋放

 keep on 繼續

 whatever 什麼都可以（表示不在乎）

Say It Differently 換種說法

Nancy So you're saying that cigarette smoking is not only hazardous to your health but also to your career.

Steve You don't want your job prospects to go up in a smoke, do you? Many companies in the United States seem to have the unwritten rule: if you want to advance, don't smoke.

Nancy Is that right?

Steve Yes, smokers are sometimes considered to be mentally weak or not in control of themselves – or in some cases just plain slobs.

Nancy I feel like I need a hole to crawl in.

Translation 譯文

Nancy 所以你說抽菸不僅對健康同時也對職涯有危險。

 Steve ▷ 妳不想讓妳的大好前程化為烏有吧？美國很多公司似乎都有「要升遷別抽菸」的潛規則。

 Nancy ▷ 是嗎？

 Steve ▷ 是的，吸菸者有時會被認為是心靈軟弱或無法掌握自己。在某些案例中，被認為粗俗。

 Nancy ▷ 我覺得我想找個洞鑽進去。

* hazardous 有危險的；冒險的
* career 生涯；職業
* prospect 前途；可能性
* go up in a smoke 化為烏有
* unwritten rule 潛規則
* advance 前進；升遷
* mentally 心理上；精神上
* in control （確實）掌握
* plain 明白地；顯然地
* slob 懶惰；粗俗
* hole 洞
* crawl in 爬進去

Answer Key 練習解答

❶ Extinguish your cigarette or leave.

❷ I've heard a rumor that several heavy smokers were let go in recent weeks.

❸ Whatever you tell me, I intend to keep on smoking.

Wellness Management

健康管理 (1)

Sample Conversation 範文

(Steve Lee becomes an exercise fanatic.)

 Paul I hear, Steve, that you've quitted smoking.

Nancy Not only that, but Steve has started taking aerobic classes.

Paul That's a very difficult language to master, I suppose.

Nancy No, no. I am talking about his physical fitness program, not Arabic.

Paul Oh, I beg your pardon. But I thought only young girls did that sort of thing, You know, in tights.

Steve Do you have to see my pink leotard to believe that I'm actually doing it? Joking aside, three quarters of my class are middle-aged men.

Paul Is that so? What time do you start?

Steve At 7:15 in the morning. We do aerobic dancing for 45 minutes. Three times a week. Then I can take a sauna, shave and still get to the office by 9. I've discovered this new lifestyle and I like it immensely.

Paul It must be quite stimulating for you.

Steve Yes, not only physically but also mentally. I can do more work now with less fatigue, and I sleep like a baby every night.

Translation 譯文

（Steve Lee 變成運動狂。）

Paul　Steve，我聽說你戒菸了。

Nancy　不僅戒菸，他還開始上有氧課程。

Paul　那該是相當難學的語言。

Nancy　不，我說的是健身課程（aerobic），不是阿拉伯語（Arabic）。

Paul　噢！對不起，但我以為只有年輕女孩上那種課，你知道穿著緊身衣的那種。

Steve　你一定要看到我穿粉紅連身運動衣才相信我的確在上課？笑話放一邊，我班上四分之三的人都是中年男人。

Paul　是嗎？你幾點開始？

Steve　早上 7:15。我們跳 45 分鐘的有氧舞蹈，一週三次，接著我去洗個蒸氣浴、刮鬍子而且還有足夠的時間 9 點到辦公室，我非常喜歡我發掘的這種新生活方式。

Paul　對你來說一定很令人振奮。

Steve　是的，身心都是。我能做更多事又比較不會疲倦，而且我每晚都睡得像小嬰兒一樣。

Words & Phrases 詞彙片語

● fit 健壯的；合適的；合身的

● fanatic 狂熱者；入迷者

● aerobic 有氧的；增氧健身的

- master 精通；熟練
- physical fitness 健身課；肌力與體能訓練
- program 程序；節目；計畫；安排
- Arabic 阿拉伯文
- Beg you pardon 請原諒（做錯事時）；對不起（沒聽清楚時）
- sort of 類型；形式
- tights 緊身衣
- leotard （舞蹈體操）連身運動衣（原為一名空中特技表演者 Jules Leotard 在表演時所穿著的緊身運動衣所衍生而出）
- aside 放在一邊
- quarter 四分之一
- middle-age 中年
- sauna 蒸氣浴，桑拿浴
- shave 刮鬍子
- lifestyle （有品質）生活形式
- immensely （口）非常；很；廣大地
- stimulating 激勵的；刺激的；振奮人心的
- mentally 精神上；心理上
- fatigue 疲勞；疲乏

▌A reminder 小提醒

「not only...but also」是英語中最常見的連接詞，用此連接詞所連接的字、片語或子句較強調後者，如連接兩個主詞時，動詞需與後者一致：

Not only you but also he is in the wrong.

他和你一樣都有錯。

若用「as well as」或「no less than」時,則強調前者;若連接兩個主詞,動詞需與前者一致:

Baseball is played by girls as well as boys.

女孩像男孩一樣打棒球。

The teacher no less than the students longs for a holiday.

老師和學生一樣渴望假日。

Exercise 練習

利用括弧所提供的字來寫句子:

❶ I'm talking about his physical fitness program, not Arabic.

（mean, wellness, the Arabic）

❷ Do you have to see my pink leotard to believe that I'm actually doing it?

（convince you, show, do I have to）

❸ Joking aside, three quarters of my class are middle-aged men.

（75 percent, in their forties, seriously）

Say It Differently 換種說法

 Steve You see, those who exercise regularly enjoy greater resistance to fatigue and illness. And they have a lower incidence of heart and arterial problems and lower levels of cholesterol and blood pressure. You should try too, Paul.

Paul But 7:15 is too early for me. Is that really the best time to do the workout?

 Steve It really depends on your lifestyle. At my gym, many people exercise during the lunch hour, turning it into a time of very light snacking or simply avoiding food.

Translation 譯文

 Steve 你知道嗎，固定運動的人對疲勞和疾病較有抵抗力。他們發生心臟和動脈性毛病的機率較低，膽固醇、血壓也較低。Paul，你也該試試。

Paul 但 7:15 對我而言太早了，那真是最適合做運動的時間嗎？

Steve 完全看你的生活型態而定。在我的健身房，很多人在午餐時間做運動，讓午餐變成輕食，甚至於避開食物。

✳ regularly 有規律地；定期地

✳ resistance 抗力；阻力

✳ incidence 發生率；影響範圍

✳ arterial 動脈的；幹線的

✳ level 水平；程度；等級

✱ cholesterol 膽固醇

✱ blood pressure 血壓

✱ workout 鍛鍊；練習

✱ gym 健身房；體育館

✱ snacking 吃點心零食

✱ avoid 避免；躲開

Answer Key 練習解答

❶ I mean his wellness program, not the Arabic language.

❷ Do I have to show you my pink leotard to convince you that I'm actually doing it?

❸ Seriously, 75 percent of my class is men in their forties.

Wellness Management

健康管理 (2)

Sample Conversation 範文

(Steve Lee strikes rich.)

Paul I've asked Steve to join us in discussing our anniversary project because I've just learned he's a health fiend.

Steve I can tell you that living a healthy lifestyle will become more and more important for business people.

people Overweight, overanxious, chain-smoking executives will no longer be tolerated.

Paul I couldn't agree with you more. In many companies, health is more than a personal matter. It's an organizational objective and a management issue. Health-promotion programs are considered a long-term investment in human resources. In view of this, we've come to the conclusion that we want to inaugurate a health-related movement as part of our anniversary celebration. Steve will give us the details.

Steve Our idea is to kick off an incentive health-promotion program, tentatively called the "Wellness Challenge." Its main purpose is to encourage ongoing exercise, initially by our employees. The program will pay employees $10 for each "unit" of exercise they report. One unit is, for example, jogging 1,500 meters, swimming 200 meters, bicy-

cling 5,000 meters or aerobic dancing for half an hour. That means, in my case, I can get four units or $40 per week through aerobics.

Paul　Right.

Translation 譯文

（Steve Lee 發財了。）

Paul　我發現 Steve 是個運動狂，所以我要求 Steve 加入討論週年慶計畫的事。

Steve　我可以告訴各位有個健康的生活型態對生意人來說會越來越重要。

people　過重、過度焦慮、老菸槍的經理人將不再為大家所接受。

Paul　你說得很對。在很多公司，健康不再是個人的事。它是個企業目標和
管理課題。提升健康被視為人力資源上的長期投資。有鑑於此，我們
決定要在週年慶時正式展開一個和健康相關的活動，Steve 會告訴我們
細節。

Steve　我們的計畫是要開始一個提升健康的激勵活動，初步定名為「向幸福
挑戰」。它主要的目的是要鼓勵持續的運動，先從公司員工開始，這個
活動將會以員工上報的運動「單位」為基準，每單位付員工 10 美元。
舉例說，一單位是慢跑 1,500 公尺、游泳 200 公尺、騎自行車 5,000
公尺或半小時的有氧運動。就我而言，那意思是我做有氧運動每週可
以得到 4 單位或 40 元。

Paul　對。

Words & Phrases 詞彙片語

- strike rich 發財了
- fiend 狂；迷
- overweight 過重的
- overanxious 過度焦慮的
- chain-smoking 菸一支接著一支抽
- no longer 不再
- tolerate 容許；忍受
- can't agree with you more 再同意也不過
- objective 目標；任務
- issue 問題
- long-term 長期的；長程的
- investment 投資
- human resources 人力資源
- in view of 有鑑於此；考慮到
- come to the conclusion 做出結論；決定
- inaugurate 開始；展開；就職；就任
- health-related 和健康相關的
- incentive program 激勵計畫
- tentatively 暫時地；實驗性地
- purpose 目的；意圖
- encourage 鼓勵；促進；激發
- ongoing 進行中的

- initially 最初；開始
- unit 單位
- jog 慢跑

A reminder 小提醒

「can't agree with you more」的翻譯若譯成「無法同意你」那可真是大錯特錯！就好像「You can say that again.」如果聽到他人這樣回你，你就重複你剛說的話，那又要鬧笑話了！這兩個表達都是代表「所言中的，深得我心」。

另外，如「ongoing 前進」、「onlooker 旁觀者」，「onset 開始」、「onrush 突擊」等字都是由動詞片語（動詞＋介系詞）所衍生出來的單字。類似的字還有「off-putting 不高興」、「inbuilt 內建的」、「incoming 進來的」、「intake 攝取」、「outlook 展望」等。

Exercise 練習

利用括弧所提供的字來改寫句子：

❶ Living a healthy lifestyle will become more and more important for business-people.

(it's becoming, increasingly, to live)

❷ We've come to the conclusion that we want to inaugurate a health-related movement.

(our conclusion was, we'd , kick off)

❸ Its main purpose is to encourage ongoing exercise, initially by our employees movement.

(it aims at, regular, starting with)

* kick off 開始（某事）；開始（比賽）
* movement 活動；運動
* aim at 針對；以…為目的；瞄準

Say It Differently 換種說法

 Paul I don't mind doing exercise in the evening.

 Steve They say that exercising after work often proves an effective way to relieve fatigue and give vent to built-up tension. But if you're going to exercise after a meal, you ought to eat lightly. Anyway you should find the time best suited to you.

 Paul I hurt my ankle jogging a few months ago.

 Steve My aerobics instructor says jogging is not for everyone and you shouldn't pursue it if it produces pain or injury. Walking vigorously is a good way to maintain your fitness.

Translation 譯文

 Paul 我不介意在晚上運動。

 Steve 有人說工作後運動可以有效地消除疲勞並能發洩累積的壓力，但如果你在餐後運動，你就該少量地進食。不論如何，你該找出最適合自己的時間。

 Paul 我幾個月前因慢跑而傷了腳踝。

 Steve 我的有氧教練說慢跑未必對所有人都適宜，而且你有疼痛或受傷時就不該繼續。精神抖擻的步行也是一種維持健康的好方法。

✱ prove 發現；證明

✱ give vent to 發洩

✱ relieve 消除；減輕

✱ built-up tension 累積的壓力

✱ lightly 分量少地；清爽地

✱ suit 適合；合身；適應

✱ ankle 腳踝

✱ instructor 教練；教員；大學講師

✱ pursue 繼續；追求

✱ injury 傷害；損害

✱ vigorously 猛力地；精神活潑地；有活力地

Answer Key 練習解答

❶ It's becoming increasingly important for business people to live a healthy life-style.

❷ Our conclusion was we'd kick off a health-related movement.

❸ It aims at encouraging regular exercise, starting with our employees.

Wellness Management

健康管理 (3)

Sample Conversation 範文

(Getting rich fair and square.)

Paul How will you monitor what people actually do?

Steve We won't. It should be an honor system. There'll be a monthly mini-mum. Participants will be paid only if they accumulate over 30 units per month. We also plan a cap of five units a day.

Paul I see. That'll eliminate the weekend athletes. But I'm not sure if I care for the idea of cash rewards. Personally, I'd prefer special gifts or company-paid trips.

Steve The public relations department has carried out a quick internal survey. It seems that as many as four-fifths of our people are interested in taking part in such a program, and the majority would prefer cash incentives.

Paul That's fine with me. Where do you go from here?

Steve Through the mass media, we'll communicate the message to other companies and encourage them to join the league. I'm fairly confident that we'll be able to generate a lot of publicity because of the unique-ness of the program. At the same time, we'll prepare literature on how to organize in-house wellness programs. Copies should be made avail-

able free of charge. Then we can position our company as the pioneer in corporate fitness programs while generating public goodwill.

Paul　It sounds like a good image-builder. I like it.

 Translation 譯文

（大家一起變有錢。）

Paul　那你要如何監督大家有沒有實際做到呢？

Steve　我們不監督。它是個榮譽制度，將有每月最低要求。參加者每個月必須累積到 30 單位才能拿到獎金，我們同時也將規定一天 5 單位的上限。

Paul　原來如此，這樣就可以排除那些週末（玩票的）運動員。不過我覺得現金獎勵這個主意似乎不是很好，就我個人而言，我比較喜歡特別禮物或公司招待的旅遊。

Steve　公關部門曾進行過簡單的內部調查，似乎五分之四的人有興趣參加這樣的計畫，而其中大多數選擇要現金獎勵。

Paul　這我沒意見，那之後你們的計畫如何？

Steve　我們將透過大眾媒體的宣傳，將這訊息告知其他公司，並鼓勵他們共襄盛舉。我確信我們會因為這項獨特的計畫而吸引大眾的注意。同時，我們也準備一些小冊子，說明如何籌畫各種公司內部的健康計畫。這些冊子將免費提供給需要的人。然後我們就可以把我們公司定位成企業健康計畫的先驅，吸引民眾的善意回響。

Paul　聽起來這將會有助於建立我們公司的形象，我喜歡這個計畫。

Words & Phrases 詞彙片語

- fair and square 公平的；光明正大的
- monitor 監控；監視；監聽
- honor system 榮譽制度
- monthly 每月的；每月一次的
- minimum 最小量；最低限度；最低消費
- participant 參與者；關係者
- accumulate 累積；積聚
- cap 限制；覆蓋
- eliminate 消除；排除
- weekend athlete 週末運動員（指偶爾運動的人）
- cash reward 現金獎勵
- company-paid 公司出錢
- public relations department 公共關係部門
- carry out 執行；實行；進行
- internal 內部的
- survey 調查；檢查；測量
- as many as 多達
- four-fifths 五分之四
- take part in 參加
- majority 多數；大多數；過半數
- incentive 誘因；動機；鼓勵
- go from here 後續做法

- through 經由；透過
- mass media 大眾媒體
- communicate 傳達；表明
- league 聯盟
- generate 造成；產生；形成
- publicity 宣傳（效用）
- uniqueness 獨特性；唯一性
- at the same time 同時
- literature 宣傳印刷品；文獻；文學作品
- organize 組織；安排
- in-house 公司內部
- copy 副本；份
- free of charge 免費
- pioneer 先驅；先鋒
- goodwill 商譽；友好
- image-builder 形象塑造

◀ A reminder 小提醒

「four-fifths」是分數，用分數時，分子要用基數（one, two, three...）而分母要用序數（first, second, third...）。若分子大於 1 時，分母要加「s」：

> 三分之一 – one-third
> 三分之二 – two-thirds

另外，daily、weekly、monthly、bimonthly、semimonthly、yearly 這些字可當形容詞也可當副詞：

> Most people in the U.S. receive their paychecks bimonthly.
>
> = Most people in the U.S. receive their bimonthly paychecks on the 1st and 15th of each month.
>
> 大多數美國人一個月拿到兩次薪水。

但 annually、biannually、biennially、semiannually、triennially 則指可以當副詞用，若要當形容詞用必須去掉 ly。

Exercise 練習

利用括弧所提供的字來寫句子：

❶ That'll eliminate the weekend athletes.

(sometime, will be out, that way)

❷ At the same time, we'll prepare literature on how to organize in-house wellness programs.

(produce pamphlets, structure, simultaneously)

❸ Copies should be made available free of charge.

(free copies, distributed)

✹ pamphlet 小冊子；活頁文宣

✹ structure 組織；構成；安排

✹ simultaneously 同時地

✱ distribute 分發；分配；分布

☀ Say It Differently 換種說法

Paul Using part of the $8 million of our annual budget, we ought to buy a corporate membership in a major sports club.

Steve Good idea. Also, how about organizing a weight-loss competition among teams of employees as part of the wellness program?

Paul How do you do it?

Steve The combined weight of a team of, say, five employees would be measured at the outset. Then the competition is which team loses most weight in a given period of time.

Paul Weight loss implies eating less. That would be a wonderful idea.

◖ Translation 譯文

Paul 運用我們每年八百萬的預算，我們應該可以把一家大型健身房的企業會員資格買下來。

Steve 好主意，還有，在員工團隊之間舉辦個減肥比賽來當作健康計畫的一部分如何？

Paul 你要如何做？

Steve 假如說一隊有五名員工，一開始時，先量團隊總體重，接著看哪隊在一定時間內減掉最多體重。

Paul 減肥意味著少吃，那將是個好點子。

* annual 年度的

* budget 預算

* membership 會員資格

* major 主要的；重要的；一流的

* weight-loss competition 減肥競賽

* combined 聯合的；共同的

* say 假設

* measured 測量；斟酌

* outset 一開始；最初

* given 指定的；假設的

* period （一段）時間；時期

Answer Key 練習解答

❶ That way, the sometime athletes will be out.

❷ Simultaneously, we'll produce pamphlets on how to structure in-house wellness programs.

❸ Free copies should be distributed.

A Job Well Done

做得好！

 Sample Conversation 範文

(Steve Lee is going through the year-end evaluation with his boss.)

 Paul I owe you an apology, Steve, for not getting around to your performance evaluation sooner. It's not that I had forgotten about it. On the contrary, your future career path with us has been one of the matters uppermost on my mind these past couple of months.

 Steve Honestly, Paul, I haven't minded waiting, and I certainly appreciate your concern.

 Paul As you can see on your appraisal form, I've given you a rating of "outstanding" in all three major areas of accomplishment: customer relations, sales effectiveness, and business development. You know, I really have to commend you on an all-around excellent performance. The only problem I had in doing your appraisal is that I couldn't think of anything to put down under "evaluation of results not achieved." You've accomplished everything expected of you, and more.

 Steve I must say that I think you're being too generous, especially on the last score. I've committed a blunder or two in the business development area, if you recall.

 Paul Oh, you mean the deal you initiated with the Korean trading company

that turned out to be a hoax? Listen, Steve, my philosophy is that it's far better to try many times and accept some failures along the way than only to go for the sure things. It's like baseball, where the batters with the best home-run records also strike out more than the other players. As far as I am concerned, that Korean flap isn't even worth mentioning on an appraisal sheet.

 Steve　But aside from specific cases like that, I also feel inadequate about myself in a number of respects, especially my ability to communicate in English.

Translation 譯文

（Steve Lee 正在和他老闆完成他的年度考核。）

 Paul　我為沒有早點抽空做你的考核向你說抱歉，並不是我忘記了。恰恰相反，你在我們公司日後的發展是我在過去幾個月裡最掛心的一件事。

 Steve　老實說，Paul，我不在乎等待，而且很謝謝你的關心。

 Paul　就如你在考核表上所看到的，在顧客關係、銷售績效以及業務拓展三項主要業績上，我都給你「傑出」的等級。你知道，我真的得誇獎你這樣全方位的優秀表現，我在做你考核時的唯一問題就是，在「未能完成」項目中該如何下筆，你完成所有人對你的期望，甚至還超出許多。

 Steve　我得說我覺得你太寬厚了，特別是在最後項目的分數上。如果你回想一下就會記得在業務拓展上，我曾經犯過一兩個錯誤。

 Paul　哦，你是指上回你主導和韓商做生意，後來卻發現那是個騙局的那次嗎？聽著，Steve，我的哲學是與其只做有把握的事還不如多方嘗試，

在過程中或許有失敗，但仍是值得的。就像棒球一樣，全壘打次數最
多的打者也是被三振次數比其他人還多的人。就我而言，韓商談判失
利一事在這張考核表上根本不值得一提。

 Steve 　可是，除了這種比較具體的事例外，我覺得自己在好些地方也有所不
足，特別是我的英語溝通能力。

Words & Phrases 詞彙片語

- go through 完成；經歷；熬過
- year-end evaluation 年終考核
- owe 欠；歸功於
- get around to 找出時間／機會去做
- performance 績效；表現；表演
- not that 不是
- on the contrary 恰恰相反；不是 … 而是 …
- career path 職涯規劃
- uppermost 最主要的；最高的
- honestly 老實說；誠實正直地
- appraisal form 評估表
- rating 等級；評估
- outstanding 傑出的；重要的；顯著的
- major 主要的；重要的；一流的
- area 領域；地區；範圍
- accomplishment 成就；才藝
- commend 稱讚；讚賞；推薦

- all-around 多才多藝的；全能的

- excellent 優秀的；卓越的

- put down 寫下；放下

- achieeve 完成；實現；贏得

- generous 寬厚的；大方的；仁慈的

- commit 做（錯事）；犯（罪）

- blunder 錯誤；失策；疏忽

- recall 回想；召回

- initiate 開始；創始；發起

- turn out 事實證明；結果是

- hoax 騙局；惡作劇

- philosophy 哲學

- far better 更好

- along the way 在前進的道路上；沿途

- go for 爭取；去拿

- sure thing 有把握的事

- batter 打擊手

- home-run 全壘打

- strike 三振；打擊

- as far as I am concerned 就我而言

- flap 不安；恐慌

- specific 特殊的；特定的；具體的

- inadequate 不充分的；不適當的

- a number of 若干；一些

- respect （某）方面

A reminder 小提醒

「a number of」和「the number of」是兩個完全不同的用法：

> A number of students came for the lecture but the number admitted was only 50.
>
> 一些學生來聽演講但准許入內的人數只有 50 人。

「a number of」後習慣與複數名詞連用，所以其後需用複數動詞；「the number of」後則須與單數動詞連用。

「all-around」為美式用法，英式英語多以「all-round」來代替；「around-the clock（二十四小時）」在英式英語中也會改成「round-the-clock」。

Exercise 練習

利用括弧所提供的字來改寫句子：

❶ I owe you an apology.

(apologize, must)

❷ You've accomplished everything expected of you, and more.

(delivered the goods, more than)

❸ I've committed a blunder or two in the business development area, if you recall.

(made a couple of errors, I may remind you)

✽ deliver 遞達；發表

✽ deliver the goods 履行諾言；不負眾望

✳ error 錯誤；誤差

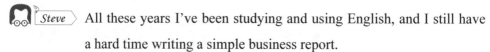

Say It Differently 換種說法

Steve > All these years I've been studying and using English, and I still have a hard time writing a simple business report.

Paul > Listen, there are plenty of businessmen and -women in the United States who can't even write a decent letter. You do a lot better than some people I could name at headquarters...

Steve > It's nice of you to say that, but...

Paul > Sure, Steve, you still have some room for improvement in that area. But given your diligence and the present level of your skills, I'm sure you can make good progress in your writing if you set your mind to it.

Steve > Maybe I should get myself some formal training.

Paul > That might not be a bad idea.

Translation 譯文

Steve > 我學英文用英文也這麼多年，但要我用英文寫出一份簡短報告還是有困難。

Paul > 聽著，就算在美國也有許多生意人，男或女，無法寫出像樣的信。你比總部裡我知道的某些人還要好很多。

Steve > 謝謝你的美言，但 …

Paul > 當然，你還有改善的空間。但在你的勤奮和現有技術水準的前提下，只要你專心去做，我相信你會有很大的進步。

 Steve   也許我該去參加些正式課程。

 Paul   這想法不錯。

* decent letter 像樣的信
* name 列舉；提名；命名
* room for improvement 改善的空間
* given... 在 … 的前提下
* make progress 進步
* set one's mind on 下決心
* formal 正式的

Answer Key 練習解答

❶ I must apologize to you.

❷ You've more than deliverd the goods.

❸ I've made a couple of errors in the business development area, if I may remind you.

From Good to Better

精益求精

(Steve Lee found out that he wasn't perfect after all.)

 Paul   Now we're getting into the area of professional skills. I've rated you "outstanding" in analytical skills, planning and organization, technical expertise, and assertiveness and initiative. For verbal and written communication skills and flexibility, my rating is "excellent" or "fully satisfactory." What I'm saying basically is that you have a good command of English but you may need to learn how to write more concisely and effectively. You might want to look into training programs in that area. Otherwise, though, I see no reason for you to feel "inadequate" in any way.

Steve   Well, the first year I was with the company, I really felt I was learning fast, absorbing knowledge like a dry sponge, and that I was applying my new knowledge to my work pretty successfully. But now I feel that my learning curve is rising much slower.

 Paul   That's only natural. The easiest gains always come first. You shouldn't let yourself get discouraged on that account. There's an old proverb that says, "Be not afraid of going slowly, be afraid only of standing still." I'd suggest that you might take it a little bit easier. Having said

that, I should also admit that I realize you may be frustrated by the lack of attractive career opportunities for you at our company.

 Steve Actually, you're right. I enjoy hard work and responsibility, and I feel a sort of obsession for excellence, if I may say so. But looking at the operation here, I realize that my career will probably plateau in, say, three to five years' time. In all honesty, I may want to look for new challenges at that point.

Translation 譯文

（Steve Lee 發現他畢竟不是那麼完美的。）

 Paul 現在我們來看看專業技能這一部分，在分析技巧、計畫、組織、技術性專業知識、決策力和創造力上，我都評為「傑出」。至於口頭和書面溝通技巧及適應性上，我給的是「優秀」或「十分滿意」。基本上我要說的是，你的英文能力不錯，不過，你需要學習如何才能寫得更簡潔更有效率。你也許會想找些這方面的訓練課程，除此，我看不出你有什麼理由覺得自己「有所不足」的。

 Steve 是這樣的，在公司的第一年，我真的覺得自己學習得很快，吸收知識的速度就像一塊乾海綿一樣，而且，我能很成功地把新知識應用到工作上。但現在我覺得我學習曲線上升的速度慢了許多。

 Paul 這是自然的啊！先學的總是最容易的，你不該因為這樣就感到喪氣，有句俗話：「不怕走得慢，就怕不前進」。我建議你別把這事看得太嚴重，說了這麼多，我其實也知道你可能會因為我們公司無法給你什麼有吸引力的工作機會而沮喪。

 Steve 實際上，你說得對。如果可以的話，我喜歡艱難的工作和身負重任的感覺。我對優秀有點著迷，可是看到這裡的工作情形，我了解到我的事業可能在三、五年之內就會停滯不前了。我坦白說，也是這個原因我想另尋挑戰。

Words & Phrases 詞彙片語

- from good to better 好還要更好
- professional 專業的；職業的
- analytical skill 分析能力
- technical expertise 科技專長；科技知識
- assertiveness 果斷；武斷
- initiative 主動性；進取心
- flexibility 彈性；適應力；靈活性
- satisfactory 令人滿意的；符合要求的
- good command of 能駕馭；精通
- concisely 簡明扼要的
- otherwise 否則；要不然
- no reason for 沒理由
- absorb 吸收；汲取；理解
- sponge 海綿
- learning curve 學習曲線
- only natural 必然的
- gain 獲益；利潤
- discouraged 沮喪的；氣餒的；灰心的

● account 記述;理由;帳(戶)

　on that account 那件事上

● stand still 停滯不前

● frustrated 挫敗的;失意的;洩氣的

● lack of 缺乏

● attractive 吸引人的

● obsession 著迷;沉迷

● plateau 停滯期;高原

● in all honesty 誠實地;實在地

● challenge 挑戰;質疑

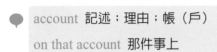
A reminder 小提醒

「realize」中的字尾 ize 在英語中通常代表動詞:

formalize: 形式化、criticize: 批評、jeopardize: 陷入危險;危及、
hospitalize: 入院

在日常商務運作中,有許多未必為大家接受但在商業上卻是已經習慣的用法:

prioritize: 決定先後順序、finalize: 定案;完成、normalize: 正常化、
incentivize: 給予獎金、privatize: 民營化

英語中有許多用法,雖未合乎文法規定,但在實際使用中卻廣為大眾所接受。通常這些才是我們要格外留意的。

Exercise 練習

利用括弧所提供的字來改寫句子：

❶ I see no reason for you to feel "inadequate."

(there's, "not capable")

❷ You shouldn't let yourself get discouraged on that account.

(don't let, discourage you)

❸ In all honesty, I may want to look for new challenges at that point.

(to be honest with you, change in my career)

✱ capable 有能力的；能幹的；有才華的

Say It Differently 換種說法

 Paul All in all, Steve, I'd say you're a real quick study. You seem to pick up new information so fast that it doesn't surprise me that you find your pace of absorption slowing down after a while.

 Steve Well, I guess if you look at it that way...

 Paul Another area where I have to rate you highly is your ability to respond to criticism in a constructive manner.

 Steve Actually, I hate being criticized but I hate even more letting myself get irritated by it. So I try my best to accept it if it's valid and modify my opinions or behavior accordingly.

 Paul If only everybody in the office would take that approach!

Translation 譯文

 Paul 總之，Steve，我覺得你是個學習能力很強的人。你似乎能很快學會新資訊。所以，在一段時間後你覺得吸收速度變慢也不意外。

 Steve 我想這是我現在的想法…

 Paul 另一個我給你高分的考核項目是你能用建設性的方式來回應批評。

 Steve 老實說，我恨被批評，但我更恨讓我自己因受到批評而變得急躁。所以我儘量把批評變成合理的並據此修正我的看法或行為。

 Paul 真希望辦公室裡所有人都能這樣做！

* all in all 總而言之
* respond 做出反應；回答
* constructive 建設（性）的
* irritate 惱怒；煩躁
* modify 修改；緩和
* opinion 看法
* accordingly 因此；於是；相應的
* approach 方法；方式；態度

Answer Key 練習解答

❶ There's no reason for you to feel "not capable."

❷ Don't let that discourage you.

❸ To be honest with you, I may want to look for a change in my career.

Relocation?

調職？

Sample Conversation 範文

(Steve Lee is offered a chance to start fresh again.)

Paul I'm sure that a highly marketable young individual like you will have no trouble findning job offers, if you haven't received some already.

Steve I'd be lying if I said I hadn't. Right now I don't think I'm ready for a change. There's still so much I want to learn about this business. But I also recognize that sooner or later I'm likely to run into a career block within this company.

Paul Steve, I think that's a highly realistic assessment of your own prospects with this company, if you stay in Taiwan, that is.

Steve Could you explain what you mean by that?

Paul Sure. What I mean is that you should experience an oversea assignment to keep from falling into a rut here. It would broaden your horizons, and it should also unblock your path to further advancement within the organization. Based on some earlier conversations we've had, I've recommended you for a transfer to Corporate Marketing in New York. The official approval just came in this morning. Congratulations, Steve.

Steve I, er... thanks, Paul.

 Paul　The assignment will be for a period of at least three years. You'll be exposed to various phases of our business in the States, and eventually you can expect to return here as a key member of our management team. I'm sure you'll get a lot out of it, and I'm confident that you'll enjoy it too.

 Steve　This is so sudden, I don't know exactly what to say. But I really appreciate your support, and I'll do my best to live up to your expectations. Anyway, thank you.

 Paul　Don't thank me, thank yourself. You earned it.

Translation 譯文

（Steve Lee 有了新開始的機會。）

 Paul　我確信像你這樣搶手的年輕人要找到新工作機會絕非難事，搞不好已經有人向你接頭了。

 Steve　如果說沒有，我就是在騙你了。不過我不覺得我準備好要換工作了，在這行中還有許多我需要學習，但我也體會到我早晚會在公司裡遇到生涯瓶頸。

 Paul　如果你還想待在臺灣的話，我想你如此評估自己在公司的前途是相當實際的。

 Steve　你的意思是？

 Paul　我的意思是為了不讓你在這陷入一成不變的刻板生活，你該去經歷海外派遣任務，海外歷練會拓展你的視野而且也會打開你日後在公司升遷的管道。根據以往我們的談話，我已經向公司推薦把你調到紐約的

行銷部門，今天早上已收到正式的批准。恭喜你，Steve！

Steve 我…謝謝你，Paul。

Paul 這次的派遣至少三年，在美國你將會接觸到公司的各個層面。最後你會回到這裡成為我們管理階層的重要幹部。我確信你會有很大的收穫，你一定會喜歡的，Steve。

Steve 這事太突然了，我不知道該說什麼，但我真的謝謝你的支持，我也會盡最大努力以符合你的期望。總之，謝謝你。

Paul 別謝我，謝謝你自己，這是你該得的。

Words & Phrases 詞彙片語

- relocation （舉家）遷徙；遷置
- marketable 暢銷的；有市場的；市場的
- individual 個人；個體
- recognize 承認；識別；認出
- sooner or later 早晚
- block 障礙；區
- realistic 現實的；逼真的
- assessment 評估；估價
- prospect 前景；展望
- oversea 海外的
- assignment 任務；派遣
- rut 老套；慣例
- broaden 拓展；擴大
- horizon 眼界；範圍；地平線

- unblock 解除障礙
- advancement 晉升；前進
- transfer 調動；轉移
- corporate （總）公司的
- official 正式的；官方的
- approval 批准；認可；同意
- a period of 為期
- at least 至少
- various 不同（種類）的
- phase 階段；時期
- eventually 最後；終究
- key 重要的；關鍵的
- sudden 突然
- do one's best 盡全力
- live up to 符合；做到
- expectation 期望；期許

◀ A reminder 小提醒

「lying」是「lie」的現在分詞，英語中動詞的時態變化如果是不規則的，一定要特別小心：

> lie（說謊）– lied – lied – lying
>
> lie（躺）– lay – lain – lying
>
> lay（放置；生（蛋））– laid – laid – laying

hang（懸掛）– hung – hung – hanging

hang（吊）– hanged – hanged – hanging

die（死）– died – died – dying

dye（染）– dyed – dyed – dying

在上述例字中，各種變化不一，和單純的規則變化（在字尾加 d、ed 或 ied）相比，不規則變化要複雜許多。

Exercise 練習

利用括弧所提供的字來改寫句子：

❶ I'd be lying if I said I hadn't.

(have to admit, have)

❷ You can expect to return here as a key member of our management team.

(be a key player on, after you)

❸ I'll do my best to live up to your expectations.

(all I can, disappoint you)

✱ key player 關鍵人物

✱ disappoint 失望

Say It Differently 換種說法

 Paul Oh, one more thing, Steve.

 Steve Yeah?

 Paul ⟩ I do hope you won't have to leave your family behind when you go to the States, the way so many Taiwanese businessmen seem to these days.

 Steve ⟩ Well, as you realize, the children's education tends to be a paramount concern for a lot of people. They're afraid that their kids won't be able to get into good schools if they spend too long abroad.

 Paul ⟩ That strikes me as rather sad.

 Steve ⟩ I agree. Personally, I think it's good chance for children to be exposed to a different culture. I'll have to discuss this with my wife, but I'm almost positive she'll want us all to go together.

Translation 譯文

 Paul ⟩ 對了，Steve，還有一件事。

 Steve ⟩ 嗯？

 Paul ⟩ 當你去美國時，我不希望你像大多數的臺灣商人一樣把家人留下來。

 Steve ⟩ 如你所知，孩子的教育是多數人的第一考量。他們擔心如果在海外待太久，孩子就無法進到好學校。

 Paul ⟩ 這讓我感到有些感傷。

 Steve ⟩ 我同意，就我個人而言，我認為這是讓孩子接觸不同文化的好機會。我會和我太太討論，但我深信她會要我們全家一起去。

✽ paramount 最高的；最重要的；卓越的

✽ abroad 在國外；到國外

✽ strike 猛然想到；打擊；攻擊

✱ sad 悲哀的；糟糕的；遺憾的

✱ be exposed to 暴露在 …；接觸到 …

✱ positive 確定的；有自信的

Answer Key 練習解答

❶ I have to admit I have.

❷ After you return, you can expect to be a key player on our management team.

❸ I'll do all I can do to not disappoint you.

作　者　Alan Bond
　　　　Nancy Schuman
書　號　1AG0

即選即用英文商業書信(增訂二版)

新時代全方位的商業書信參考書！
翻開書就會寫商業書信！

　　各種形式的商業溝通，舉凡洽詢函、投訴信、道歉信、祝賀函、商業通知信、邀請函、下訂單、授信文書、催繳函、求職信、履歷表、會議紀錄、商業報告及提案、傳真、電子郵件，本書都有最適合的範例提供參考，並配合書信解說及常用句單元，詳細解說寫作目的，方便讀者套用替換，輕鬆掌握商業書信寫作技巧。

作　者　李普生
書　號　1AH3

餐飲英語

　　藉由訂位、迎賓、服務、點餐、進餐、烹飪、甜點、速食、抱怨、買單等單元，提供學習專業、正式而禮貌的商業英語措詞，以及了解餐旅業之專有名詞與常用之服務對話內容，進而將所學之餐旅英語實際應用於職場之中。

全書分為14篇，每篇以6單元呈現：1.課文、2.詞彙、3.情境對話、4.句型介紹、5.文法重點、6.練習，並明列各式飲料菜名菜單及烹飪方法的用字，以及與餐飲相關的資訊，提供學習者更多、更完整的知識。

❖推薦書單❖

作　者　李普生
書　號　3AG0

超簡單英文文法速成

一本完全針對臺灣人學習英文的習慣來規劃編寫的文法書！

本書依據作者教授臺灣人英文多年的經驗，將不易弄懂的文法，搭配圖表解說，加深讀者的印象。每個章節之後囊括各項考試必考的文法觀念，設計題型並附加詳細的解答，讓讀者不需要死記硬背就能輕鬆學好文法。

作　者　李普生
書　號　3AL0

超實用生活英語分類單字

生活、工作、運動、看病要用的單字這裡通通有！

本書以中文情境分類方式列出生活中常用的字彙，內容涵蓋食、衣、住、行、育、樂等，讓讀者迅速查找臨時需要的單字並擴充字彙，除了能以聯想式記憶法記憶單字，更是一本可隨身攜帶、隨時查閱的工具書。

國家圖書館出版品預行編目資料

即選即用商用英語會話／李普生著. ― 初
版. ― 臺北市：五南, 2015.08
　　面；　　公分.
ISBN 978-957-11-8193-6（平裝）

1.商業英文　2.會話

805.188　　　　　　　　　　104011585

1AG6

即選即用商用英語會話

主　　　編 ― 李普生(81.7)

發 行 人 ― 楊榮川

總 編 輯 ― 王翠華

主　　　編 ― 朱曉蘋

責任編輯 ― 吳雨潔

封面設計 ― 吳佳臻

出 版 者 ― 五南圖書出版股份有限公司

地　　　址：106台北市大安區和平東路二段339號4樓

電　　　話：(02)2705-5066　　傳　　真：(02)2706-6100

網　　　址：http://www.wunan.com.tw

電子郵件：wunan@wunan.com.tw

劃撥帳號：01068953

戶　　　名：五南圖書出版股份有限公司

法律顧問　林勝安律師事務所　林勝安律師

出版日期　2015年8月初版一刷

定　　　價　新臺幣400元